Sabine Baring-Gould

Through Flood and Flame

A novel

Sabine Baring-Gould

Through Flood and Flame
A novel

ISBN/EAN: 9783337412203

Printed in Europe, USA, Canada, Australia, Japan

Cover: Foto ©Andreas Hilbeck / pixelio.de

More available books at **www.hansebooks.com**

THROUGH FLOOD

AND FLAME.

A Novel.

IN THREE VOLUMES.

VOL. III.

LONDON:

RICHARD BENTLEY, NEW BURLINGTON STREET,

Publisher in Ordinary to Her Majesty.

1868.

Book II.—FLAME.

(*Continued.*)

CHAPTER VII.

FOR a few weeks Annis felt the difficulty of falling into a position which she had been unaccustomed to occupy, and to find entire ease in the society of Miss Furness. There was something in that lady which filled her with awe, at the same time that she was attracted powerfully towards her. Miss Furness was different from those ladies with whom she had hitherto been brought in contact. There was in her a repose, an inherent dignity and grace, which was new to Annis.

She possessed qualities which the girl had
never observed among the well-to-do manu-
facturers' wives and daughters in Sowden.
This aroused Annis's wonder. She watched
her intently, to find out what was the exquisite charm in her, that she might acquire
it herself. But that same charm she herself
unconsciously possessed. It was naturalness.
In Miss Furness there was no affectation,
no self-assertion, no effort to appear other
than she really was. All her acts were
spontaneous, springing from the impulses of
a disciplined heart and a refined head.

She drew Annis towards her, and unconsciously impressed and moulded her. The
girl continually and involuntarily contrasted
the monied aristocracy of Sowden with the
lady whom she now daily saw. They wore
their gentility as though it had been made
by a bad tailor and did not fit; they were
constantly engaged in looking it up, and

asserting it; in proclaiming it by their expensive dress, in announcing it by costly
plate, in forcing it into notice by their dash-
ing equipages, in repeating it in their gilded
furniture, in assuring people of it in their
conversation. Their gentility had no braces
to keep it up. It slipped down, and had to
be pulled up with a jerk, and then directly
after was descending, to be again hitched up;
it was never stationary, it was always in
process of slipping down or of being brought
up with an effort.

Annis's life in York was very calm and
monotonous; one day passed much like
another. Mrs. Furness had to be dressed
every morning, to be fed, to be argued with
touching her nose-tubes; had to be given her
course of psalms and lessons, and amused
till the early dinner hour at half-past one.
In the afternoon, if the weather were fine,
the old lady was wheeled in a chair round

the Minster yard and close. At four, Miss Furness and Annis went to service in the Cathedral, and at six had tea. Then the old lady was put to bed, supplied with her tubes, and sent to sleep with a chapter.

During the evenings Annis worked with Miss Furness, reading to her, or being read to: these evenings she thoroughly enjoyed.

The girl was happy. She was fond of both the old woman and her daughter, she enjoyed the quiet of the little house, the solemnity of the great Minster standing before the windows, sending its mighty shadows over the houses, its great bell booming at the hours, the organ thundering within, and heard indistinctly without. The gravity of the cathedral town, after the stir and noise of a manufacturing village, impressed her; and the numerous vestiges of antiquity around her opened up to her peeps into long vistas of history of which she had

no conception before, and which awoke her
liveliest interest, and kindled her enthusiasm.

She never tired of the Minster. Whenever she was able, she ran into it, or
wandered round it. The battered pinnacles,
the corroded tracery, the disfigured statues,
were full of charm to her. She watched the
birds fluttering about the parapets, and soar-
ing to the towers, with a longing to be like
them, prying incessantly into the mysteries
of stonework of that vast fabric. Within,
the screen of the kings delighted her beyond
expression, and she was convinced that each
statue was a portrait. She loved to unravel
the confusion of the venerable stained
windows, and pick out a bishop here, and
an Adam and Eve there. The great dragon
in the triforium of the nave, stretching its
gaunt neck over the passers-by, filled her
with awe; the little sparrows on Archbishop Grey's tomb delighted her con-

tinually. The numberless heads in the transepts, grinning, yawning, crying, proved of inexhaustible interest ; so too was Delilah clipping Samson's hair, whilst the strong man rent the lion over the aisle door. From the ghastly emaciated John Haxby, lying behind a grille, she ever shrank with horror.

In Mrs. Furness's house Annis found abundant matters of interest. The curiosities which had been collected by the Silver Poplar seemed to her never to exhaust themselves. When she thought she had seen all, Miss Furness would open a drawer, and display exquisite tropical shells and sea-weeds, which she had not hitherto cast her eyes on. Or the lady would unlock a cabinet, and produce a collection of Egyptian idols, and fragments of a painted mummy case. The admiral's library was also there, consisting of voyages and travels to all parts of the globe, full 'of pictures, many coloured.

The little girl often thought of Hugh and Martha. Sometimes a feeling of longing came over her to be back in Sowden at the factory, reeling, but then the remembrance of the misery of that last day there returned and stifled the longing.

Mr. Furness often wrote to his sister, and sent her kind messages, telling her news about Sowden, and her cousin, but never mentioning Hugh. And now and then Martha put in a little note, hoping that it found Annis as it left her (Martha), in good health.

So time passed by. Christmas came, and the streets of York rang, like those of Sowden, with the strain,

"Christians awake, salute the happy morn!"

chanted by a choir, bellowed by schoolboys,

whistled by carriers, ground from a hand-organ, played by a German band, trolled out of tune by drunken men, till every soul in York was sick of being bidden "awake, and salute the happy morn," not in the early part of the day, but more especially towards dusk of evening, and vociferously at night.

Christmas in Yorkshire is a time for noise and merriment. Then the streets are thronged with parties of mummers endeavouring to obtain admission into peaceful households, where they may cause uproar; or sword dancers seek turfy lawns on which to perform the play of St. George; or the yule tup bursts into kitchens, frolicking and kicking, and only to be pacified with cake and ale. Then by night and by day children prowl about with "milly-boxes," containing a Virgin and child, surrounded with oranges and coloured bows, craving a

little offering to adorn the box, in the
pretty words of a pleasant carol :—

> " We go a wassailing
> Among the leaves so green."

And after the round of " milly-boxes " is
over, comes the more serious round of Christ-
mas-boxes ; boxes for coals, boxes for ringers,
boxes for lamplighters, boxes for water-
carriers, boxes for porters, boxes for errand-
boys, boxes for milkmen, boxes for butchers'
men, boxes for bakers' men, boxes for every
one. Indeed, any person for whom a job,
however trifling, has been performed during
the past twelvemonth, a job which has been
paid for and is fondly deemed done with, is
boxed. No one with a little money at his
disposal escapes being boxed ; ladies suffer
most, being boxed without the smallest
compunction, boxed in their own houses,
boxed on their doorsteps, boxed in the street,
boxed even in church.

Christmas is unquestionably a joyous time—to the boxers; but it is a season of trial of temper and emptying of purses to the boxed.

There is little fear of those old English customs dying out which give opportunity for extortion of money.

One beautiful day after Christmas Miss Furness and Annis were walking on the city walls, which at York form a delightful promenade for two, but an aggravating one for three. After having made the circuit of the lower part of the town, they stood leaning on the parapet and looking at the turbid Ure.

"I miss them mountains and hills we had at Sowden," observed Annis.

"Do not say them," Miss Furness said; " say those, instead."

" Those mountains," the little girl repeated.

" I dare say you do feel the want of them, my dear," Miss Furness now answered. " The neighbourhood of York is very dull and flat. But then it has its charms. There is the river Ure."

" There is a river at Sowden," said Annis ; " it is not quite so big as this one, but it is a fair-sized river for all that."

" It is black or blue with dye."

" Ah, Miss Furness, and this is brown with mud."

" Well, if you have a river at Sowden, you have not got a Minster."

" No," answered Annis ; " that indeed we have not. I never thought I should see so bonny a building—may I say bonny ?" she suddenly asked, looking cautiously up.

" Yes, by all means. It is a beautiful word, and far more expressive than pretty. I do not think you will venture to compare your Sowden factories with the cathedral."

"No, I should not think of doing so. But I do miss the hills."

"My dear," observed Miss Furness, "you will find, all through life, that you are losing some things and gaining others. Remember, that if we are to be happy, and to profit by what falls out, we must not repine over those things which are lost, but keep a look-out for the things we are to gain. I hope you are not fretting over your removal from Sowden."

"Oh no, no, Miss Furness!" answered Annis, flutteringly. "I hope you have not thought that. You have been so very, very kind to me, and I am so happy and comfortable. I would not for the world have you think that I was fretting."

"Dear child, I know that your heart must turn at times to the old friends, old scenes, to memory dear: it is only natural."

"I did love Sowden," said Annis, musing.

" And those there," added Miss Furness.

" And *some* of those there," was the girl's correction.

" Of course you could not love all," the lady said, laughing.

"Oh, Miss Furness!" Annis began. " I do wish my cousin Martha knew you, and you knew her. She is one of them girls——"

" Those."

" Of those girls who never do aught but what is right. Martha always knows what is best to be done, at any time, choose how great a difficulty——"

" One moment. That expression, ' choose how,' is peculiar. Suppose you alter the wording a bit. There, Annis, you will think I am always catching you up."

" Thank you for doing it. I want to speak right."

" I think you had better alter that

sentence into, ' however great a difficulty she may be placed in.' "

" Very well, Miss Furness. Now I will say it——"

She suddenly paused.

" What is the matter, dear?" asked Elizabeth Furness after a while.

"Oh! do look yonder. Do you see that strange figure ?"

" Yes," answered Miss Furness, looking in the direction indicated.

" I suppose you mean that stoutish, thick-set woman."

"Do you see her veil?"

"She has her head turned. Yes. A red veil."

" I have seen that woman in the street, and in the Minster, and she always wears her veil down. And, besides, it is such an odd colour for a veil—is it not?"

" It certainly is an unusual colour."

" Have you observed her when she walks ?"

" No, I did not notice her before this minute."

" Her walk is strange. She is queer altogether. When she is by, I cannot take my eyes off her, and—" Annis dropped her voice—" I can't but think she is looking at me through her red veil all the time of service at the Minster. I fancy I see her eyes glitter. And when I pass her——"

" Nonsense, Annis."

" Please, Miss Furness, I can't help it, so don't be angry."

" I am not angry."

" No, but I am afraid you will be when I say something. But I must say it. I am frightened of yon woman."

" Has she spoken to you ?"

" No, but I think she follows me."

" Perhaps she wants assistance; she is

evidently poor. Shall I go up to her and speak."

" No, no, no !" anxiously catching Elizabeth's arm. The woman, who had been on the walls, now left them abruptly.

"Why should she wear that red veil always down?"

" Perhaps the poor thing suffers from a complaint in her face," answered Miss Furness.

Annis shuddered. Some memory was recalled by these words.

" Let us go home," she said. " I hope I shall never see her face."

CHAPTER VIII.

"AND now, if you please, let me hear the particulars."

"Of what, uncle?"

"I am clear as to the manner in which you got out of the water, but I am imperfectly acquainted with the manner in which you got into it. One or two facts are obvious. You did not plunge into the canal of your own accord; the man with whom you took the dive must have cast you in, and he must have had some reason for so treating you. Explain."

"You ask me to do that which is entirely beyond my power," answered Hugh.

" How so ?"

" Because I am in the dark as to the cause, unless that be the simple one of insanity."

" Who threw you into the water ?"

" That raving maniac, Earnshaw, your watchman."

" Was he in the train with you ?"

" He was. He attacked me furiously with a knife. Look at my hand ; there are the evidences. Then he grasped me in his arms, and leaped over the bank with me into the canal. Uncle, I told you some while ago that the man was mad."

" It certainly looks as if he were mad ; madder, I mean, than the majority of people. Most folk do not job at others with knives. The usual practice is to use the tongue for that purpose, and a much more damaging weapon that is than knife or stiletto. Most folk do not either jump with others into canals. They usually prefer to involve them in some desperate speculation. Go on."

" What more am I to say ?"

" I want the reasons why this madman singled you out for attack. Why did he not attempt to murder me instead of you ?"

" I believe he bears a dislike to me."

" Why so ?"

" How can I tell, uncle."

" Because you must be perfectly aware of the reason of this dislike. Nothing, my dear Hugh, goes on in this world without a reason. No effects are produced without causes. Why did Earnshaw dislike you ?"

Hugh hesitated for some while. At last he said frankly—

" I believe he has taken my engagement to heart."

" Petticoats !" with a burst, like the explosion of a gun. " Always petticoats."

" I should like to know," said Hugh, "whether the fellow has turned up, alive or dead."

" No. He has not. The police have been making inquiries. The bargeman saw him sink, and is strongly impressed with the conviction that the man is drowned. His body has not however been recovered as yet, notwithstanding that the drag has been used, and that a loaf weighted with quick-silver has been floated on the canal——"

" What, sir ?"

" Ah ! you do not understand. When a body is lost in a river or canal, it is the custom here for a penny loaf, with six-penn'orth of mercury in it, to be launched on the water. Popular superstition avers that the bread will remain stationary over the spot where the corpse lies."

" And has this been tried ?"

" Certainly. The bargeman conducted

the experiment before a great concourse of interested and expectant people, but without result."

"Earnshaw wore a thick, heavy, great-coat, which, when sodden, must have weighed heavy, and, if he is drowned, will retard his rising."

"That he is drowned, I have very little doubt. The peculiarity of his appearance would certainly have attracted attention if he had landed and made off. I shall have to get a new watchman, and a fresh set of keys, for Earnshaw has carried down with him those of the warehouse and factory. He had duplicates, so as to be able to let himself in at night in case of fire. These are now probably in his great-coat pocket, in the slime of the canal bottom."

"It will be well to ascertain whether he really is lost."

That can only be done by letting off the

water of the canal, leave to do which is costly, as it retards traffic. To my mind, the negative evidence is as strong as the discovery of the body would prove. For, consider, a man with a face marked in the frightful manner that his is, must be observed wherever he goes. He will need shelter and food, and if he enters shop or lodging, his features at once attract attention; and the police are notified to be on the look-out for a man so disfigured."

" If Earnshaw does turn up alive, he must be put into a lunatic asylum."

" *If* he does.   But I• suspect he will trouble you no more. Now look in the paper, and see what a muddle has been made of your little adventure."

" Where. I should like to see."

" There. Next to that account of the robbery at Midgeroyd."

" What has taken place there ?"

" Oh, only a cottage broken into, and clothes stolen from it."

This conversation took place in the office. Hugh had completely recovered the effects of his immersion, but his hand was still inflamed and sore from the cut of the watchman's knife.

The paragraph in the ' Mercury ' was this:

" SOWDEN. ENCOUNTER WITH A MADMAN. On Friday evening Mr. Arkwright, the son of a well-known manufacturer of Sowden, was attacked in a second-class carriage on the Lancashire and Yorkshire line, between North Dean Junction and Sowden, by a maniac armed with a knife. The encounter was of the most desperate character; and Mr. Arkwright, having been already severely wounded in several places, threw himself out of the carriage into the canal which adjoined the line of rails, and succeeded in reaching the other side in safety. The madman, however, in springing after him, struck the embankment, as it appears, and was stunned, for, having rolled into the water, he did not rise, though the spot where he had fallen was anxiously watched, both by the gentleman he was pursuing, and a barge-man who happened to be close at hand. As yet, the body has not been recovered. The deceased, whose name was Joseph Earnshaw, has long been considered of unsound mind, but had not been regarded as dangerous. Mr. Arkwright, who was promptly attended by a surgeon, is con-valescent, none of the wounds being mortal, though one was within a hair's-breadth of a vital centre."

"I think," said Hugh, laughing, "that the purveyor of information for the 'Mercury' in this neighbourhood has been as near the truth as was the wound to a vital centre in me."

Then he ran his eye over the next paragraph.

" MIDGEROYD, NEAR SOWDEN. On the night of the 30th, a lone cottage belonging to a somewhat eccentric old lady in the hamlet of Midgeroyd was broken into by some ruffians, who carried off wearing apparel, having first consumed the contents of the good woman's larder. The burglars made so little noise that the old lady did not discover her loss till the following morning. It is probable that they anticipated finding money, but were disappointed. The police are confident that the perpetrators of this outrage belong to a band of professional thieves, who have for some while infested the neighbourhood of Halifax, which is their head-quarters."

"Do you know anything of the poor creature who has been robbed?" asked Hugh.

"Yes, a little," answered his uncle. "It is old Peggy Lupton, a lone woman who is popularly regarded as a miser, and who is actually a poor creature who has known better days, and who finds it a hard matter to make both ends meet."

"I see. One of those mysterious individuals we are made acquainted with by advertisements under the ghastly title of decayed gentlewomen. For my part I have never seen one. I have shrunk from the sight, supposing it to be revolting."

"Peggy is a good woman, and somewhat eccentric withal. She lives quite by herself in a lonely place. But Gretchen can tell you more about her than I can, for she visits her occasionally, and gives her a little assistance in the shape of a pound of tea or sugar, and odds and ends of clothes. You may depend upon it, before long, Mrs. Lupton will be hovering about our door, full of woe, and throwing out hints that she is short of dresses on account of the robbery. I have seen the poor woman equipped in a complete suit of your aunt's old clothes. There was an old familiar green tartan I was very fond of, and to which I had become so accustomed, that I looked to see the tartan at tea every bit as truly as I looked for muffins and cake. One day my wife appeared in a different gown. I remonstrated. She assured me she had given away the green tartan; and, sure enough, next Sunday Peggy Lupton turned up in church, wearing the identical gown I had grown to love. It was exasperating."

"And now the green tartan is in the possession of the thieves?"

"I should not be surprised. By the way, I wonder whether something else has gone."

" What, sir ?"

" Something about which Gretchen and I have had many a joke; indeed, at one time, almost a quarrel. She brought with her from Germany a quantity of foreign articles of apparel, which would do well enough in Deutchland, but which are quite out of place in England. Among other articles of this sort was a veil. On the continent people indulge in extraordinary colours. They have crimson and blue umbrellas, whilst we never rise above green. I have seen Frenchmen in burnouses lined with scarlet, the hood displaying its colour as prominently as one belonging to an Oxford M.A. The ladies are not content to veil their faces with black, blue, or green, but affect red; and one Sunday, of all days, your aunt appeared in church with a carmine veil. I secreted it on my return home, but she found it again. I protested against its use; she declaimed against

English want of appreciation of colour. I vowed I would burn that veil if I found her in it again. She entreated for it, and at last we compromised matters by her giving it to Peggy Lupton. Now, Hugh, shut up your book and come along. We must be home early to tea, as the Doldrums are expected."

" I am ready, uncle."

" What do you think of Laura, eh?"

" She is a very nice, unaffected girl, and good-looking as well."

" And she has lots of money. Keep your eyes open. The secret of success in life lies in being always alive to opportunities, and seizing them as they occur."

Laura really was, what Hugh said, a nice, unaffected girl; and she was also decidedly good-looking.

She had dark hair, a rich brown skin, with cheeks that glowed warm and luscious as a peach, bright, dancing, hazel eyes, full

of life and light, a faultless figure, and
an elastic step. Laura was never grave.
She woke with a chirp in the morning, and
went chirruping to bed at night. Her
mother plied her with coffins, and she
danced over them; she impressed on her
shrouds, and she laughed behind them; she
regaled her with funerals, and they got into
her head and made her giddy. Yorkshire
people are supplied with an almost inexhaustible supply of animal spirits. In this
they are distinguished from the Lancashire folk, whose calm, saddened tone, is in
marked contrast to the exuberant mirth of
the good people east of Blackstone Edge.
In a Lancashire town you meet pale, earnest
faces, bowed heads, and eyes full of intel-
ligence, but no sparkle. In a Yorkshire
town you are startled by the gushing vitality
that boils up on all sides. The "loosing"
of a Lancashire mill is a different thing alto-

gether from that of one in Yorkshire. From
the former, the hands steal away, silent,
thoughtful, and depressed; from the latter
they burst away in an effervescing, palpi-
tating flood, noisy with laughter, and song,
and joke, and glowing with leaping blood
and bubbling spirits.

Laura had enough vital energy in her
to supply a whole Lancashire family. The
day was too short for expending it. She
flooded her mother with her vivacity, and
then plunged down into the kitchen, where
she speedily excited an uproar. Then she
darted into the town, paying visits or shopping, and letting off a little of her spirits
wherever she went. This excess of life in
one unrefined or uneducated becomes very
generally vulgarity. Had Laura not lady-
like instincts, and had she not been at good
schools, she would have been set down as a
giddy, boisterous tomboy. As it was, she

never degenerated into vulgarity, and never descended to real improprieties.

Mrs. Doldrums was a woman of no education or natural refinement : she had few interests, and those few were centered in mortality and smoke-jacks. Deceases and the subsequent interments were the principal subjects of her thoughts ; but mortal diseases, as conducing ultimately to death and a funeral, presented subsidiary attractions. Smoke-jacks, as having led to her fortune, were not without their charms in her eyes, and she could descant on the merits of her husband's patent with vehemence if not eloquence. Adonis spent half his year with Venus in heaven, and the other half with Proserpine in Hades. Mrs. Doldrums also in thought shared her time between a sublunary and a subterrestrial world. The upper world was that of the smoke-jack, the lower world was that of the mouldering Doldrums. Now, the old lady was in body with the smoke-jack, then, she was in spirit with the deceased.

But Laura, by having been sent to school, was elevated to a sphere sufficiently removed from the smoke-jack, and infinitely remote from the mouldering Doldrums.

In society the mother was not brilliant. She was wont to sit and smile, and turn her rings on her fingers, and wipe her brow with a handkerchief, perfectly silent, till some casual remark, more or less remotely connected with smoke-jacks, bereavement, or decease, fell in her way, when she rose with a rush, burst in on the conversation, expanded, became dogmatic and noisy. then collapsed and settled down to the bottom once more, waiting for another rise.

Mrs. Doldrums affected a title. This title was, "The Relict." It was one of which she was proud. Providence, she was

wont to say, not royalty, had made her the
Relict of Jonathan Doldrums. To circumstances, not to ancestry, she owed this
honourable distinction. Some had obtained
titles by a career of crime, she by the over-
ruling hand of destiny.

Mrs. Doldrums was a bad reader, a worse
writer, and an abject speller. A consciousness of her defects made her profess ocular
debility, which no spectacles could relieve.
Accordingly, she shrank from reading,
shunned writing, and revolted against spell-
ing.

The stout lady's ideas were not harmonized
by what the schoolmen call the grace of
congruity. They were accustomed to fuse
together distinct conceptions into a com-
pound far less valuable than the famous
Corinthian brass; and when she did read her
newspaper, or when she heard it read to
her, she rose from it with a general con-

fusion of ideas as to the localities of the
battles, the objects for which armies fought,
and the sides on which the generals were
engaged. And when the element of Court
of Probate and Divorce, and again, that of
royal movements, were imported into the
news from the seat of war, Mrs. Doldrums'
conception of the state of politics was one of
inextricable confusion, in the midst of which
gleamed a single prominent spot of red—
General Garibaldi.

Laura Doldrums made no attempt to
conceal her admiration of Hugh. The
romance attaching to him had invested him
with a charm in her eyes, equal to that
characterizing the conventional hero of a
novel. She cared the less to hide her
admiration, because she regarded him as engaged, and therefore carried beyond the reach
of her love. Had he been free, she would
have been more cautious in exhibiting her

appreciation of him ; but as he was secured, she felt as if all necessity for masking her devotion was obviated. Hugh, on the other hand, was flattered. It was impossible for any one to dislike Miss Doldrums, and when a young man feels that he is attractive to a pretty, bright, and amiable girl, he cannot fail to be fascinated. Hugh did find pleasure in her society, and he did not object to let his feelings be known.

Young people of opposite sexes are shy of one another as long as there exists a possibility of their becoming united. The girl thinks that the man is struck with her, and intends to make an offer, when he shows an approach to familiarity ; and he, on his side, is ever on his guard lest she with whom he is brought in contact should suppose, by his throwing aside restraint, that he entertains ulterior designs. But when this cause of mutual distrust is removed, they frankly

and readily form friendships of a simple and
guileless nature, such as that which exists
between brother and sister, beautiful and
mutually beneficial, and of which each
through life preserves a hallowed remembrance.

Mr. Arkwright was highly pleased to
notice the regard for one another exhibited
by the young people; and he fondly hoped
that this regard would ripen into attachment, which would in turn mellow into
love. But Laura was not one to whom
Hugh could have devoted heart and soul.
Her liveliness attracted, but did not capti-
vate him; her elasticity of spirits pleased,
but did not fascinate; he was amused by
the sparkle of her mirth, but he feared lest
it should evaporate and leave flatness behind.
He observed in Laura abundance of vivacity,
but felt the deficiency of repose. Those men
who ally themselves to companions full of

fire and steam, are by nature dead weights, but most men prefer being the engine to the tender on the railroad of life.

On the return of Mr. Arkwright and his nephew to their house, they found the Relict of Jonathan Doldrums and Laura already arrived. The little German lady had involved herself into inextricable confusion in attempting to make an explanation to Mrs. Doldrums of the method of cooking spinach with sugar in her own country. And that lady, believing that the conversation turned on politics, was descanting on General " Garibawldy," whom she regretted to find involved in a sad divorce case, on account of Herr Bismark's attachment to the infamous singer, Chassepot, an affair which was likely to result in dividends to the ritualists.

" Don't, mother !" deprecated Miss Doldrums.

"My dear, remember my eyes are not what they were. I have consulted the most eminent oculists in Halifax and Bradford, and they all agree that I must mind my eyes; that they want humouring, and that I am not to exert them."

"Yes, mother," persisted Laura; "but surely your eyes did not pursue the General into Austria, and bring him to bay in the Dividends."

"My dear, I assure you it was all in the papers. I read it myself, and Sally read the rest to me. The ritualists are in arms, marching upon Rome, and General Garibawldy is at their head."

"Garibaldi!" exclaimed Hugh. "You amaze me, ma'am."

"Yes, sir, Garibawldy is an eminent ritualist. He wears a scarlet vestment, and if that ain't being a ritualist, I don't know what is."

" And marching against Rome ?"

" No, no! you misunderstand me. Count Bismark, of Alipa— Laura, what is it ?"

"Oh, Henry," interrupted Mrs. Arkwright ; " what do you think ? I have had one visit, and from whom ?"

" I cannot tell.

" Guess, Henry, guess."

" Count Bismark, or the ritualist Garibaldi ?"

" But no. From the old woman, Mistress Lupton."

" Did not I tell you so ?" asked Mr. Arkwright, turning to Hugh, with a laugh.

" It is true she has been robbed."

" Yes, I am aware of that. I saw it in the paper."

" Poor thing. It is schrechlich! and she is affrighted all over. The robbers stole the most of her habiliments, and she is quite ill of the fright. They ate up her beautiful pie, and they drank her beer, and they took away her habil—— "

" Enough of that word!"

" What shall I use ?"

" Clothes is the proper term."

" You taught me of the other.   Well, es geht nichts! what think you they have taken ?"

" The pie."

" Ah ! yes, but besides."

" The beer."

" That is very well, but still more."

" Why, the habiliments."

" The clothes, sir.   And of them ?"

" I never enter into particulars, especially when the articles belong to a lady."

. " Why, Henry, the veil, the red veil. That is gone also."

CHAPTER IX.

ONE evening Annis was standing in the nave of York Minster, listening to the organ voluntary after the service. The gas in lines of light below the triforium, and the nine jets above the altar, filled the choir with a soft yellow glare; but outside the great screen of the kings all was dark, except that a flake of light fell through the screen gates, and a subdued twilight hung about the intersection of the nave and transepts. The five sisters were like plates of frosted silver. A faint glimmer stole through the rich tracery of the western window; the nave pillars were scarcely distinguishable.

Annis stepped into the south aisle, where she might stand unobserved, and drink in, in silent rapture, the rolling music of St. Cecilia's instrument. The organist was playing "Despairing, cursing rage," from the Creation, and he made the old walls quiver with the thunder of the great fugue. Annis was completely abstracted, and did not notice the choristers clattering from their vestry to the transept door; nor observe the minor canon stalk past with hat and stick, complacently stroking his light whiskers; nor the blind gentleman feel his way, tapping the pavement with his staff; nor the old women disappear, hawking and coughing. Annis had a genuine West Riding love of music, and the great organ in the Minster excited her daily delight. Hitherto she had only heard the singing of the church choir of Sowden, and its small instrument. There was a magnificence in

the great organ of the Minster which over-
whelmed her.

The throbbing of the serried waves, the
quivering of the walls, and the shiver of the
glass suddenly ceased, and the exquisite
chant, "A new created world," floated
through the dusky Minster, and thrilled the
little girl's whole being with rapture.

When a hand was laid on her arm she
scarcely noticed it, so entranced was she,
and it was only when the flutter of a veil
before her eyes attracted her attention, that
she all at once became conscious that the
mysterious woman, for whom she had expressed to Miss Furness her aversion, was
holding her, and endeavouring to lead her
further down the nave aisle.

"Let go," said Annis, startled. "What
do you want?"

Then the organ bellowed forth once more :
"Dismay'd, the host of hell's dark spirits

fly ; Down they sink in the deep abyss, To endless night. Despairing, cursing rage, attends their rapid fall;" and it was impossible for her to catch a word of the reply in the vibrations of sound.

But as again the pure, tender melody, " A new created world," swept softly along, she heard a musical voice say, " I am very poor, I am very poor, Miss Greenwell."

" Do you want relief?" asked Annis, compassionately.

" Will you visit me ? I am very poor."

The organ had ceased. The voice of the woman with the red veil affected Annis strangely. She looked nervously and fearfully at the thick-set female figure before her, with the strangely-coloured veil drawn over the face.

" Where do you live ?"

" In Peter Lane."

" I will tell Miss Furness."

" No," said the woman, sharply. " You must come. No one else."

" I really cannot. You are mysterious. Why should you wish to see me, and not the lady with whom I live ?"

" There are reasons," answered the woman.

" All out !" bawled the verger, rapping his staff on the ground. The echoes lumbered down the aisles, and muttered in the chapels and vestries.

" You must come. Promise."

" Indeed I will not."

" All out !" again, and imperiously.

" You are hardhearted ; surely you will come and see a poor thing who is nigh clemmed."

" Miss Furness will visit you, and give you relief."

" I will have no Miss Furness. I must and will have you."

"Now then!" from the verger. "All out! All out, please."

So they were hurried towards the transept door. The white-jacketed bellows-blowers straggled past. Then the organist went out. The gas was extinguished. Down went the verger's staff with a far-echoing stroke. The transept clock ticked the hour; for the last time the verger called, vociferously and ferociously, "All out!"

All out! muttered the walls about Archbishop Scrope. Now the prelate can lie still through the long night, wrapped in contemplation. All out! whispered the slabs about the emaciated John Haxby. Now the moon will flare in on his ghastly face and skeleton limbs, and none will see him turn and laugh and grind his teeth behind his grille. All out! was called from wall to wall of the choir, and alone in the hush of night, the brass eagle will wait poised and expectant till twelve o'clock, when he will rise and sail thrice round the great church, in and out among the moon-streaks from the clerestory windows. All out! went laughing down the dark triforium of the nave, and then the dragon will turn his head, with none to see him uncoil, and he will hiss at St. George, and the Saint will smite him once, twice, thrice.

All out! faintly in the sepulchres below, telling the dead that the time of the living was over, and the time of the dead is come, when they may rise for the solemn mass of souls.

"Annis!" was spoken slowly and distinctly from behind the red veil.

The girl's blood leaped to her heart.

"Annis. I expect you to visit me to-morrow, at three, in Peter Lane."

"I——"

"You will come!" Then down the steps,

across the yard, and away into the gloom, went the stranger.

Miss Furness observed that something was wrong with Annis when she came in. She looked up from the book she was reading to her mother, and said—

" My dear, you look very white."

" Oh, do I, miss ? it is nothing."

" You have been standing listening to the organ, have you not ?"

" Yes, I have. I could not help it. The music was so beautiful."

" Well, and you have got a chill. Now come up to the fire. There, darling, kneel down on the mat, and get the roses back into the little gardens of your cheeks. We must not have winter there."

" I—wish—Annis—you—would—put —those tubes—" began Mrs. Furness, slowly, and with great effort to speak distinctly.

"Oh, fudge, mammy!" laughed Elizabeth; "you know you can't have them till
you go to roost."

Annis knelt before the fire, expanding
her hands, and musing on what had taken
place. She felt a pressure on her heart,
caused by fear; and she asked herself again
and again whether or not she should go to
Peter Lane on the morrow. She was not
in general reserved with Miss Furness, but
she could not resolve to tell her her trouble.
Bessie had laughed at Annis for being afraid
of the red veil, and Annis was too sensitive
to incur this again.

When she went to bed at night, it was
not to sleep. She turned wearily from side
to side, but could not find rest, for the poor
little mind was still revolving the same
question, Shall I go? It was strange that
such a simple matter as a visit to a poor
woman should so harass her, but the red-

veiled person was regarded by her with a peculiar and inexplicable repugnance. Whenever in the Minster she caught sight of that veil—and if it were in the church at all, she was certain to detect it at once—she could not keep her eyes off it. It fascinated her, with the fascination of horror. She was imbued with a sickening dread lest the veil should be lifted, though for a moment only. Her wakeful eyes looked towards the window where the Milky Way streaked the dark night sky with hazy light. She heard the Minster clock tell the hours, and they seemed to glide along with speed. Then the form taken by the window curtain distressed her; it assumed a resemblance to an antiquated bonnet, over which hung a veil. She turned her face to the wall with a weary sigh, and endeavoured, by counting sheep going through a hedge-gap, to trick sleep into closing her eyelids. But when she had counted till uncertainty supervened, the form of the shepherd appeared standing in the gap, wearing a rough coat and slouched hat, and she was brought to consciousness with a start, by turning mechanically in bed, fearing lest she should see his face.

Then she crept from her place, and going to the washstand, half filled the tumbler with cold water, and drank it off.

The clock tolled three. She fled to her bed, thinking that in twelve hours she was due at the house of the Red Veil.

At last a broken sleep came on, from which she woke scarcely refreshed in the morning, and still with the leaden weight upon her heart.

"I must, oh, I must go!" she said, despairingly.

Three o'clock in the afternoon sounded as Annis entered Peter Lane. It is an old, wretched, half street in the city, with totter-

ing, unpainted, unplastered houses on either
side, their windows dirty and cobwebbed,
and many broken, and patched with scraps
of newspaper.   A low public-house stands
on one side, with a broad window half obscured by a green gauze screen.   Near it is
a shop, where is sold ginger-beer in summer,
or what professes to be ginger-beer, but
looks like the wringings of dishclouts; and
in the window are unwholesome. pink and
yellow drops in bottles, which have adhered
and partially dissolved.   And on the opposite side in a window are some discoloured
eggs, and a plaster cow spotted with fly-
marks, and a small badly-written label
affixed to the glass by various coloured
wafers, which must have been moistened to
thin pulp before applied: on this label is
written, " Fresh Milk."

The houses are high, and are apparently
inhabited chiefly by children, and children

with perennial colds in their heads. Uncombed, unwashed heads of small and big " bairns " appear at the windows of the top story ; on the next below are to be heard children fighting ; on the next is to be seen a woman smacking a child on a sensitive part of its body, and the said child running, not at the nose only, but at eyes and mouth as well.

Peter Lane, having pursued a short career of dirt and disorder, suddenly shrinks into a narrow passage about three feet across, with doors opening into it, but no windows, seeing that it is too contracted to admit of much light. Across the wider, and therefore least reputable part of the lane, in that its width allows greater scope for the exhibition of its degradation, is hung a clothes line, on which are suspended articles of wearing apparel and chamber linen, which have been washed ; but these articles are

all so much out of repair, as to excite surprise that they were thought worth wash-
ing, and next, are so badly washed, that it
is only their position on a clothes line which
entitles them to be regarded as having
undergone soap and water.

Just where the lane contracts is an accu-
mulation of broken crockery, orange peel,
carrot tops, and potato parings, round
which a lean, yellow, stumpy-tailed tom-cat
is cautiously smelling. Near this spot a
fetid gutter takes its rise, a gutter which is
the principal source of amusement to the
children of the lane, for therein, from earliest
infancy, they paddle with their feet and
dabble with their hands, and over it straddle
at a maturer age, and thence derive the
major portion of the dirt with which they
decorate their persons, and especially be-
grime their noses. On this, in summer,
they float walnut-shells, and in winter

slide; into this they pour the slops of the houses, and out of this gather an abundant crop of typhus, cholera, and scarlatina seed.

It was into this lane that Annis entered, frightened, and looking from side to side. She passed the tavern and the ginger-beer shop, and was about to enter the narrowed passage, when the door of a small yellow-washed hovel, jammed in between two tall toppling houses, opened, and in it stood the woman with the red veil.

" I have been expecting you."

" I have come," said Annis, faintly.

" Come in."

The girl looked round and hesitated. The woman caught her by the wrist, and drew her within.

" Follow me."

The Red Veil went first down a low passage, leading towards the back of the house, threw open a rickety, wormeaten door, and led her into her room.

"Sit down." The woman pointed to a low three-legged stool near the fire. Annis looked about for a chair, but there was only one, and that the strange veiled female took. She pointed again to the stool, and the girl seated herself on it.

Neither spoke. The woman looked intently at her from behind her veil, and Annis leaned her cheek on her hand.

"Yes, like that," said the woman, shortly : "as of old."

That was the position in which the girl had been wont to sit in the little cottage in the sand-pit.

"You're changed, too," the woman said, after a long pause.

The room in which Annis found herself was very small and low. The house was old. The timber of the floor of the room above showed black, as there was no ceiling. By the side of the fire there was a little one-pane window, or peep-hole. The main window was in compartments, partly latticed with old smoke-tinted quarries, partly patched with square panes, " bull's-eyed " in the middle. A scanty bit of green curtain was drawn back from the window. The walls were papered with various patterns, in strips, of the most discordant colours, and all dirty, peeling off, and tattered.

Before the fire lay coiled up a white cat, very clean, on a shred of rug.

" Totts !" whispered Annis.

The cat looked up, stretched itself, and leaped on her lap ; there it coiled itself up once more.

" Do you know me ?" asked the strange woman.

" I think I do," the girl answered, faintly.

" Shall I lift my veil ?"

"No, no, no!" with a cry of distress, and a shiver which sent the cat off her lap.

"The same as ever," followed by a deep sigh. The voice had lost its musical tones, and was deep and sonorous.

"Why have you come here? Oh, why did you come?" asked Annis, with her eyes determinately fixed on the cat.

"Because I am constrained to hide."

Annis shuddered.

"You killed that dreadful man," she said.

"Yes, I killed him—him who was insulting you."

"Oh, why did you do that, Joe? But I suppose you did not mean to do it. No, I am sure it was done accidentally, and I have said nothing about it to any one. I have been so afraid of telling what I know, and getting you into danger."

"You are anxious for me?"

"Yes, Joe, of course I am. You rescued

me from that man-monkey, and I feel bound to do what I can to save you from the consequences of what followed."

" Annis."

" Yes, Joe."

" That man was a hypocrite."

" I know it. I feared and disliked him."

" Do you fear me?"

She could not answer with her lips; but there was no mistaking the meaning of the pale cheeks and nervously twitching hand, and look of the distended eyes.

" Do you dislike me?"

"Oh! do not ask me such questions. Please do not. I am very, very grateful to you for having saved me from the man-monkey. I shall never forget what I owe you for your ready help that dreadful night."

" And you will do all you can to screen me?"

" Yes, indeed I will. I have not spoken

to a soul of my having seen you in the lane that night with—— Oh! I cannot bear to think of that."

"Did you suspect me in this disguise?"

"I do not know what I thought. No, Joe; I do not think I did, till I heard your voice, and even then I was not sure. But I always felt——" She hesitated.

"Well, what did you feel?"

"I felt frightened when I saw that veil ever down."

"What has made you visit me to-day, suspecting who I was?"

"I was afraid, if I did not come, that you would be seeking me out at home."

"Home?"

"At Mrs. Furness's house, and then there might have been danger to you, as questions would have been asked, and I could not have told lies. And besides——" She broke down and hung her head.

"Go on.   And besides."

" I cannot."   Her tears burst from her
eyes, and she was compelled to give way to a
fit of sobbing.   Earnshaw did not attempt to
interrupt it, till she had herself overcome its
violence.   Then he said leisurely again—

"Go on.   And besides."

" Joe !"   She spoke in a tremulous voice.
" I should so like to know something about
my old home.   I hear so very little."

He growled in his strange beast-like manner, and began to pace the room, muttering
to himself.   She gazed at him in alarm.
He must have seen her fear, for he stopped
suddenly and asked—

" You want to know all about folks at
Sowden ?"

"Oh yes ; so much.   I have been here
many months, and heard nothing.   Tell me
something, do, pray."

" I have been here some months also."

" But when you left, were all well ?—all at the mill ?"

" Whom do you ask for especially ?"

" Martha, and Susan, and Rebecca, and Jane Foljambe."

" Yes."

" And—— Oh, Joe! Is——" She trembled, poor little bird! For four months she had not heard a word of Hugh, or been able to speak of him, and her heart ached to know something about him. But yet she dare not ask.

" Do you ask after Hugh Arkwright?"

" Yes, yes !" glad that the question was put for her. From beneath the veil proceeded a long low howl.

" I do not know," he said at last.

Spots of colour had risen to her cheeks. Now they vanished again; and her head, which had been eagerly raised, sank upon her hand.

Earnshaw strode up to her, grasped her by the shoulders, and said, in his deep, sonorous tones—

"Tell me truly, lass, do you love him?"

The little girl trembled in his powerful grasp, and, without answering, covered her face with both her hands. The disguised man did not relinquish his hold, but shook her gently, to attract her attention. She felt that his eyes were fixed upon her with an intensity of interest from behind the veil; she dared not look up and catch their glitter through the red gauze, lest she should cry out in the agony of her horror. But every nerve of her body was excited and quivering, and the pressure of the hands on her shoulders struck through her to the soles of her feet.

"Answer me," said the man.

She clasped her hands, and, looking vacantly into the fire, replied—

" I do, indeed I do. I have heard nothing of him now for many months, and I
am so anxious and troubled, that I cannot
feel happy. Do, Joe, do tell me something
about him."

" I can tell you no good."

" Joe !" plaintively, tremulously. " What
do you mean ? Is he well ?"

" I cannot say."

" Tell me this, then. Is he alive ? I fear
such things, sometimes."

" I cannot tell you even that."

" Oh, Joe ! I have such an ache here."
She laid her hand on her bosom. "I long
so much to know something about him. I
do not wish to see him, but just to hear of
him, to be sure that he is alive and well,
and happy ; and I thought you might have
been able to give me some little information.
One evening I was on the walls at dusk,
looking over the river, and I fell into a sort

of waking dream, and I seemed not to see anything; but all at once an unspeakable terror came over me, with nothing apparent to cause it. I was not afraid for myself, but I thought Hugh was in danger. I heard the scream of the engine coming into York station, and somehow, unaccountably to me, it mixed itself up with the terror that oppressed me. And then, all at once, as the whistle stopped, I became conscious of the rushing water below the walls, and I was chilled to ice, and there was a struggle within me as though I were battling with the flood, then a sharp pain in my chest, just as if I had been struck there. Yet all the while, I did not feel for myself, but for *him*. I could not sleep that night, and since then I have always had a restless fear hanging about me, and a longing to know how he is. Is it not strange, that the very day after I had that waking dream, I saw you standing in your red veil by the Minster door for the first time."

Earnshaw let go his hold of her as she spoke, and recommenced his pacing up and down the room.

" Annis," he said, " you shall know something about him shortly."

" Oh, thank you, thank you. But do not expose yourself to danger on my account."

" I want to know as well as you. But I tell you this, you shall never be Hugh Arkwright's wife."

" I do not suppose that I ever shall," she answered, sadly. " I now know better than I did what stands between us. No, I never shall be. But I must think of him still, and long to know how he is; and I shall always pray for him."

" Do you ever pray for me ?"

" Joe, I have not as yet, but I will."

" Do so."

" You will tell me something shortly about him ?"

" Yes, yes. Damn ! How you go back to *him* at every moment. You were talking of *me* last. Speak about me now."

" What shall I say ? Are you very well, Joe ?"

" I am never well with this face." He made as though he would lift his veil, and Annis, seeing the motion, quickly turned her head to the wall. Seeing this, he burst into a loud discordant laugh.

" I am going back to Sowden," he said, when his laughter ceased. " You send me to Hugh Arkwright."

" I would not have you run into any danger. I had rather that you did not go. At all events, do not wear that dreadful red veil, it unnecessarily attracts attention."

" Does it? It suits my complexion."

"Yes, but red veils are not worn now, and people are forced by the colour to notice you, when otherwise they might not give you a thought. Where did you get it?"

" That I will not tell."

" Will you wear this one instead?" asked Annis, drawing a parcel from her pocket, and opening it. " I bought this thick dark green veil for you on my way. Give me that other."

" You take an interest in my welfare."

" Indeed I do," said the girl, gently. " I could not do otherwise, knowing how grievous are your trials, and how great a service you once rendered me."

"Turn your face whilst I change veils," Earnshaw said, in a softened tone. Annis obeyed. Near the fireplace was a small square pane of glass let into the wall. This commanded the street, the main window of the room opening into a little back yard. Annis looked from the dark room into the dusky Peter Lane, whilst the red silk veil was being untied, and the green one being fastened on the bonnet.

"If you determine on going to Sowden," she said, "remember that the cottage in the sandpit is mine. It belonged to mother, and is unlet. I believe that John Rhodes has seen to its being set to rights since the flood. You can go there. Martha would be able to get the key for you; and if you tell her you do not want it to be known in Sowden that you are there, she will, I am sure, be silent. You can always trust Martha. Give her my best love, please."

"I can let myself in without the key," answered Joe. "What are you looking at so fixedly now, lass?"

"I think I saw a policeman pass the

little window, and come to this door. Hark! I hear him in the passage."

"He is come for me," said Earnshaw, composedly. "Now, lass, detain him as long as you possibly can."

They heard the voice of the officer making inquiries at the door, and the words of the lodger, who occupied the front room on the left, in answer—

"On, down yonder, you can't miss. Door on t' right hand," left them in no uncertainty of the object of the policeman's visit. Earnshaw slipped through a side door into the back kitchen, which communicated with the yard, and Annis was left in fluttering expectation.

The room was nearly dark now, but a glow from the fire illumined the floor, and the puss lay basking in it, on its side, with the legs extended. Annis drew the chair into the gloomiest corner, and sat down. She heard each step of the policeman, as he stumbled along the passage, and momentarily expected his entrance.

But just before he came to the door, Earnshaw stepped back into the room, caught up the white cat, and disappeared with it again.

The policeman rapped at the door, and Annis called tremulously to him to come in.

"Service, ma'am," with a look round the room, and a nod towards the figure seated in the shadowed corner. "Hope you enjoys middling health. I've come arter a little job, you see, and I hope there won't be no unpleasantness whatever."

"What do you want?" she asked, in a low tone.

"I want to know all about some articles of clothing, a green tartan gown more partickler, and a red veil, as was taken some few months ago from an old lady's house

near Sowden. We ain't bound to suspect
you, you know, but I happen to have observed a werry great similarity atween your
dress and them articles as was taken away
by, there's no doubt, a gang of thieves nigh
Halifax, and there are a deal of cases where
they've been at their carryings on. Now,
mayhappen we may catch 'em through that
gown and veil, if you can tell us where
you bought 'em. Some slop shop, I reckon ;
and if you say where they was got, we can
easy find out the sort of chaps who disposed
of 'em, do you see ?"

" Yes," faintly.

" I ain't going to frighten an old woman
such as you. You ain't like to be house-
breaking of a night, and burgling. That's
what men does, it ain't the province of old
women. But if men steal female garments,
it ain't their province to wear 'em, though
some men is over partial to petticoats. If

they take 'em, they dispose of 'em to a receiving shop, and the shop sells 'em. And if we find them as buys 'em, do you see, we can learn where that party bought 'em, and we can discover from the shop as sold 'em whence they got 'em. That's clear as a parabola of Euclid, now ain't it?"

" Yes."

" So now I must know all about where you purchased that tartan gown, and that red silk veil. So tell me, old lady."

" I never got them."

" How can you have the everlasting face to tell such a busted lie? When I see you with my bodily eyes in 'em, coming down Coney Street to-day and yesterday, and the day afore that. It's a wonder to me I never observed 'em before. But we're bidden look alive over those eternal thieves, and I saw the identical articles specified in the ' Hue and Cry,' which you wear every mortal day."

"I do not wear them.   You have made a mistake."

"Me make a mistake!   Not if I knows it, missis.   That ain't my province, no more nor wearing a glazed hat ain't yours. I'll just do myself the favour of showing a light."

He lit a twist of paper at the fire, and applied the flame to a tallow candle on the mantelshelf.

"There now.   I'll take a good look. Ginger and treacle!   But who are you?" staring at Annis.

"I am visiting the old person who lodges here."

"A visit of charity?" examining her from head to foot.

"Yes," answered the girl; "I suppose you may call it so.   The woman lodging here told me she was very poor, and in want, so I came to make inquiries."

" Who are you, miss, may I ask? I'm dumbfoozled with having made such a mistake."

" I live with Mrs. Furness, in the Minster yard."

" And where's the old woman ?"

" She is out."

" And are you waiting for her, miss ?"

" Yes."

" Where may she be ? Have you been waiting long ?"

" Not very long.   What time is it ?"

" Half after four o'clock."

" She generally goes to the Minster at four ?"

" You're right.   But ain't you seen her ?"

" Yes, I have seen her."

The policeman shook his head, and opening the door into the back kitchen, peered in there.   The door to the yard was locked on the outside.

The moment that the man's back was turned, Annis rose from her chair, crossed the room, and thrust the red veil between the bars into the fire.

" There's a smell of burning ; you're singeing yourself," said the policeman, on his return. " You shouldn't ought to stand so close to the fire; you'll turn your gown rusty, you will."

" I suppose I need wait no longer," said Annis, nervously.

" There's no occasion, miss. I'll make myself comfortable here till the old lady comes back from the Minster, and I'll tell her you kindly called. Miss, you *are* burning." He came over to the fire with his candle, stooped, and picked out of the grate a fragment of smouldering red silk gauze.

" I may say," said the policeman, " that this is a rum go. I believe this is a bit of that identical veil. I never saw a rummier go. I may assert, miss, without fear of contradiction, it's the very rummiest of rummy goes."

"I will say good evening." Annis made a slight bow as she glided towards the door.

" Stay a minute, miss. When did you see the old lady last ?"

Annis hesitated.

" I don't mean particular as to the minute."

" A short while before you came in."

· " And you was waiting her return ?"

" Yes."

" What made you think she was gone to the Minster ?"

" I did not say she was. I said I thought she generally went there, and that is perfectly true."

" Which way did she leave the house ?"

" She went through the back kitchen. I only saw her go in there."

" The door into the yard is locked from the outside," mused the policeman. " By Ginger! I have it, she locked the door against me. Why, miss, will you believe it! No, you hardly can, but I see right through it, from one end to the t'other. She must ha' seen me coming, and guessed what I were a coming arter. She's deeper nor I thought for, and we're diddled both of us. You'd better go home, miss, for I must make a search. Odds, ginger alive! To think I should have missed her. As I came in at one door, she hooked it out of the t'other. Hold hard!" this to Annis. " Will you tell me how long this party has been in York ?"

" About four months."

" You are sure ?"

" Yes. I first observed the person on the last day of October."

" Ginger !" he exclaimed. " To think that Me, Me, Mr. Physic, is diddled."

CHAPTER X.

THE cold damp of the morning had taken
the stiffness out of Mrs. Jumbold's curls,
and they depended on either side of her face
in elongated screws. The cold had given a
dull blue tinge to her nose, and had purpled
her lips, and reddened her knuckles. Mr.
Jumbold was supplied in the person of his
wife with a barometer and a thermometer in
one. When the weather was dry, her ringlets were short and crisp; when moist, they
uncurled and draggled to her shoulders.
The hue of her nose, lips, and knuckles was
also a sure indication of the temperature.

A cold spring rain had set in, and

Mrs. Jumbold's ringlets were faithful witnesses to the downfall, and her nose, knuckles, and lips, to the chill.

She tramped about Sowden in goloshes, with a black umbrella expanded over her poke bonnet, her gown drawn up to a somewhat unnecessary height, displaying a pair of exceedingly thin stocking-encased props, which described segments, and curves, and straight lines, and angles, about the causeway, in avoidance of little water-filled hollows. Mrs. Jumbold affected rainy days. When the sun shone, and the sky was blue, she kept much at home, but as soon as the clouds burst, and the day gave tokens of an intention to be disagreeable, the doctor's wife emerged from her door, in goloshes, umbrella, and white props, to make charity visits, to call on her acquaintances, and to do her shopping.

She was not unwont to combine the visits

to the sick and poor with those to her equals in position in one expedition, bringing, with the goloshes and umbrella, dirt and water into whatever house received her.

If she had visited a cottage in which was scarlatina, or, better, typhus, best of all, small-pox, she made a point of next visiting a friend who had children.

"I never take infection," she said to herself, "and I do not believe in it. If there be such a thing, then I am only making work for my husband."

On the day, the events of which are being now recorded, this lady called on Mrs. Tomkins, an intimate friend.

"Come, Sissy; come, Gussy," croaked Mrs. Jumbold, addressing the little daughters of Mrs. Tomkins. "Come and give me a kiss."

Then, holding the children in her arms, she said, fixing her eyes on the mother,

"Do you know that poor thing, Mrs. Bowers, in Westgate? She has four children down with measles. I have just been sitting with them. The room was so stuffy. Now— another kiss, darlings."

"Run away, run away!" ordered the horrified mother. "Gussy, Sissy! out of the room with you."

"Ha, ha!" laughed Mrs. Jumbold. "You are afraid of infection, are you? That is silly; scientific men don't believe in there being such a thing as infection. It is a superstition of the past. You need not be alarmed for the little things. Even if they were to catch measles from me, why, it is a complaint all must have, sooner or later, and the spring is as seasonable a time to be having it in as any. I always think it a good thing to get these diseases over and done with; then you know what to expect with children. You know they have good

constitutions. If they are to die, let them
die early, is what I say; then they're more
sure of going to heaven, and there is not
such an outlay in clothes, victuals, and
education. Now there was young Mr. Hall
cost his father a great amount. He was sent
to a first-rate school, and then to college; and
what did he do there? He caught scarlet
fever, and he died. That was a pity. If
he'd had scarlet fever at all, he should have
had it when a baby, and he'd have died
then, and not have cost so many hundreds
of pounds in learning Latin and Greek,
which could be of no use to him in the
other world. I'm sure, if I had children,
I'd expose them early to all the diseases
they would be likely to have, and then I'd
know their stuff. I'd know whether they
were likely to live or not, and regulate
expenditure accordingly. If I had a girl
who was weakly, and who nearly died

through measles, probably she wouldn't
survive scarlatina, and if she did, whooping-
cough would be the death of her. Now,
such a girl as that. Do you think I'd send
her to an expensive school, and dress her in
silks and satins? Not I. She should pick
up what learning she could from her sisters,
and wear her sisters' old dresses—that is
supposing the sisters were able-bodied and
vigorous, and had got through the customary
complaints without dying."

Another of Mrs. Jumbold's visits was to
Mrs. Arkwright. That little lady had just
new carpeted the drawing-room with a
delicate white Brussels, powdered with
flowers. The doctor's wife came in without removing her goloshes, and with her
dribbling umbrella still in her hand.

"Ach, weh!" exclaimed the little German
woman, after the departure of her visitor.
"What a horrid mess she has made. The

great brown footmarks, and the slop where she poked the end of her Regenschirm."

She also made a call on Mrs. Hawkes, a bride.

"Where do you suppose I have been?" asked the doctor's wife. "I have been to see that old Betty Coltman."

"We are going to have an early lunch," said the bride; "will you take some with us? It is ready in the other room."

"Thank you," answered Mrs. Jumbold; and taking her seat at table she began again. "Poor Betty Coltman's leg is very bad. A sort of abscess has formed on the shin below the knee. It looks——"

"Will you have some chicken?" interrupted Mr. Hawkes.

"It looks very angry," continued the irrepressible woman; "and there is a livid ring of purple——"

"Some wine, Mrs. Jumbold?"

" Thank you. I assure you the discharge——"

" What is the matter with you, dear ?" asked Mr. Hawkes of his bride.

"Nothing, Henry; only I have completely lost my appetite."

She also paid a visit to Mrs. and Miss Doldrums, taking Ezra Poulter, the bedridden miser, on her way.

" You have no notion," began Mrs. Jumbold, to the Relict of Jonathan Doldrums, " I am certain you have no conception of the filth of Poulter's hovel. The floor is ingrained with dirt, the ceiling is black with smoke, the windows cobweb-covered, and the furniture broken. I have only this moment come from there. Do you know ? I seldom or never visit that cottage without bringing away "—— she dropped her voice,——" vermin."

" What !" with horror, " F ?"

" No," with solemnity, " **B.**"

" Good heavens !"

" Fact. Awful, isn't it?" shivering and shaking her dress about the floor. " I may have them about me now."

" You really mean B ?"

" I really do mean B. I should not mind F so much, but B !"

As soon as Mrs. Jumbold was gone, Mrs. Doldrums rang the bell.

" Sally, I must have the carpet examined and swept all round that chair. I wouldn't have one—— Laura !" with a cry.

" What, mamma ?"

" I think—I think--I think——"

" What, what ?"

" I am sure—yes, I am sure——"

" Oh, for heaven's sake, what, what, dear mamma ?"

" I—I— I feel one now."

" A what, mamma ?"

" A B !"

A pause. Laura stared at her mother. Sally, with her broom in her hand, stood and stared at both.

"So do I !" cried Laura, turning white.

Another pause.

"So do I !" screamed Sally.

Down went the broom, and all three fled to their respective bedrooms.

On her way home from Doldrums Lodge, Mrs. Jumbold stepped into the shop of Mrs. Rhodes.

"It is very wet, ma'am," observed that person, coming from the little kitchen at the back, into the shop.

"I should not mind the wet, but that it splashes," said Mrs. Jumbold. "I can keep it off with my umbrella when it comes down, but I can't keep it off when it splashes up. I think the paving of the town, and the laying of the causeways, is shameful."

"It is not so good as it might be," said Mrs. Rhodes. "What may I serve you with to-day, ma'am?"

"It is seldom I do my shopping in Sowden," observed Mrs. Jumbold. "I generally make a point of going into Halifax for what I want. I get things there a deal cheaper and much better than I do here. You stick on the prices in these little places, and your articles are very inferior."

"Indeed, ma'am, I think you are mistaken."

"No I'm not. I know what I'm about, and I wouldn't be shopping here to-day, only I can't get in to Halifax conveniently, and I want a penny skein of black silk."

"Anything more, ma'am?" when this was given.

"You may let me look at your ribbons."

The drawer of dark colours was exhibited,

and the lady examined them contemptuously.;

"Let me see the coloured ones, the pink and violet tints."

The drawer was produced, and its contents criticised.

"Haven't you some rather wider ribbons?"

"Yes, ma'am."

"Oh, these are too wide. Any intermediates?"

"I don't think that an intermediate width is made."

"Don't tell me that. I know better. I have seen them at Halifax of all widths. I wanted a mauve spotted with black. I see you have got none."

"Here is one, ma'am."

"Ah, but that is too wide. No, there are none that will suit. Let me look at your silk fringes."

One after another was brought out and

unrolled, but none satisfied Mrs. Jumbold;
some defect was sure to become apparent, or
the depth or shade was not to her liking.

"No," she said. "It's always the way
with your little country shops; there is
never anything in them that one wants."

Mrs. Rhodes could hardly contain her
indignation. She would probably have given
noisy vent to her wrath, had she not suddenly discovered a method of causing annoyance, in turn, to the person who had been
aggravating her.

Mrs. Jumbold had put down her penny,
in payment for the skein of black silk, and
was about to leave the counter, when Mrs.
Rhodes said blandly, with a grim smirk on
her face—

"Would you be so good, ma'am, as to let
me look at that umbrella?"

"Oh, certainly," answered the lady, pre-
cipitately, a flash shooting into her eye.

"Please to examine it. You will find it very wet. Take care; I saw one drop fall among the ribbons."

"May I ask where you got this umbrella?" asked Mrs. Rhodes, with some asperity.

"Do you happen to trace any resemblance between it and one you know?" was the return question.

"I know the umbrella," answered Mrs. Rhodes, roughly. She felt that now was her moment of triumph, and she cast aside her obsequious shop manner.

"And would you like also to claim my bonnet, my gown, or my goloshes?"

"No, ma'am. But I am pretty positive that this here umbrella belonged to us."

"Could you swear, now?"

"Yes, I am sure I could swear to it. Why, bless you, it came out of the shop; it was the only one left."

" You never sold it to me."

" No, ma'am, that I'm very certain of."

" And I shouldn't think of buying such an article as an umbrella in a little poking country village."

" No, nor buying one at all when you could have one for the taking, I fancy." Mrs. Rhodes looked triumphantly at her customer, who however returned the glance in an equal spirit of elation.

" And pray, whose umbrella do you assert this to be?" asked the doctor's wife, with a snigger.

" I know it very well," answered Mrs. Rhodes. "It belonged to our Annis, that is, Miss Greenwell."

" Indeed !" with an expression of delight which staggered her antagonist.

" Yes, this was the last black umbrella we had in stock. And after the death of Mrs. Greenwell, Annis wanted one, and we let

her have it. I could swear to it, because
Mr. Rhodes marked an A with a hot skewer
on the handle."

"There is the A!" said Mrs. Jumbold.

"And I should like to know where
you found the article, or how you got
it."

"Haven't you seen a bill put in the shop
windows, to the effect that an umbrella had
been found, and that any one who had
missed one, might recover it on applying to
me and describing the article?"

"Yes," answered Mrs. Rhodes, somewhat
discomfited. "But that was some months
ago."

"Why did you not apply?"

"Nay, I did not know that our Annis
had lost her umbrella, till I saw it, and
recognized it, in your hands. And you see
she couldn't apply because she was not in
Sowden. When did you find it, ma'am?"

"I found it the night that she left Sowden."

"Where?" with a start.

Mrs. Jumbold leaned over the counter, fixed her eyes on Mrs. Rhodes, and said, in a low, hissing whisper—

"I found it close against the heap on which lay the corpse of Richard Grover."

The woman of the shop recoiled, her face losing all its colour, and a ghastly glitter of horror appearing in her eyes.

"I was at tea that night with Mr. and Mrs. Arkwright. And when your daughter Martha came to the door, to say what she had found in the lane, I ran to the spot with the others. Whilst the body was being removed, I found this."

"Martha must ha' had it," gasped Mrs. Rhodes.

"No, she had not," answered the doctor's wife; "for I asked her, before she went

away, whether she had brought an umbrella
with her, and she answered that she had
not. You look alarmed, Mrs. Rhodes. You
really do. Come now, suppose you explain
to me how it was that I came to pick up in
Sandy Pit Lane, near the body of the man-
monkey, this article, that you have identified
as belonging to the person Annis Greenwell."

"Oh dear, oh dear! that it should ha'
come to this, and I intending all for t' best,"
moaned the terrified woman.

"I think your best course will be to offer
an explanation, or I shall feel it my duty
to place the matter in the hands of the
police."

"Pray don't call them police in. It'll
be the death o' me if they comes here, and I
a regglar chapel goer, and known to be one
of the elect. I wish I'd never listened to
what Richard said, and then it 'ud ha' never
come to this. Step inside to the parlour,

ma'am, and I'll make all clear, as far as I can. Whatever shall I do?"

Mrs. Rhodes was completely thrown off her balance. The tables had been unexpectedly turned upon her, just when she was most sure of being able to discomfit her irritating customer. She now drew her out of the shop, fearing lest what she said might be heard. The poor foolish woman was possessed with terror lest she should be brought in any way into court, and be subject to interrogations by magistrates or police. She feared lest she should lose caste in her society by such an event; for to her narrow mind the witness was every whit as bad as the criminal.

How Richard Grover had come by his death she did not know; she was aware that Annis must be acquainted with the circumstances, as the girl had not returned to the house after having been sent by her

to meet the man in the lane. She had
sufficient instinct of right and wrong to feel
that the opinion of the public, and indeed
that of her own husband, would be strongly
against her for having acted as she had
towards the poor girl, and she feared the
exposure which would bring down condem-
nation on her head.

This fear had even stifled her curiosity
to know how Grover had come by his
death.

"Oh, ma'am! I'm in a proper mess,"
began Mrs. Rhodes; "and if I tell you, you
must never breathe a word to nobody."
She paused for breath, and then continued:
" You see Richard, he were fair smittled wi'
t' girl, and he would have her brought to t'
Lord. He'd ha' converted her here, but my
master came in just as' he were agait, and
stopped t' proceedings. So Richard—eh!
he was a man o' God!—he asked me to let

him meet her somewhere, where there would be no interruption, and he fixed on Sandy Pit Lane, and I sent her there to meet him. Eh! but Richard was mighty i' the spirit, and a powerful preacher."

"Well!" exclaimed Mrs. Jumbold, "this beats everything I ever heard. Where is your conscience, madam?"

"I did it all for t' best. I was longing to see Annis a child o' grace, and there was no other way of fashioning it. I couldn't get her to chapel, no road."

"And what took place when they met?"

"Nay, ma'am, how can I tell? I never saw our Annis from the moment she left our house to meet Mr. Grover. She never came back no more, from that day to this."

"Did she go of her own accord to see the man?"

"Nay, not altogether."

"Are you sure she went there?"

"Ay, I think I may be sure o' that. I made as though it were Mr. Hugh had asked to see her once more. And she was keen enough to meet him, I reckon."

"And do you mean to tell me that she never returned?"

"She never came back. And where she is now I do not know. My master, I fancy, does, but he won't let out to me. The vicar told him; but I haven't been able to screw it out of him anyways, and I've tried a deal o' times."

Mrs. Rhodes, who in the shop had spoken fair English, in her agitation had fallen into broad Yorkshire brogue.

Mrs. Jumbold was much surprised at the revelation that had been made, and great was her internal exultation, but now she carefully refrained from exhibiting it. She had kept the umbrella by her, and had used it continually, in the hopes of its attracting someone's attention, and of her being led to some discovery thereby ; and now that the discovery was made, it was imperfect, but such as it was, it surprised her beyond measure, so utterly at variance were the disclosures with her own anticipations. She had not produced the umbrella at the inquest on the body, partly because it was a very good new umbrella, and would be serviceable to herself, but chiefly because she thought it would be more likely to lead to results in her hands than in those of the police, who would advertise the discovery as suspicious, and put the owner of the article upon his guard. She had caused a notice to be printed and put in shop windows, announcing her having a found umbrella in her possession ; and when months passed, and these notices had produced no claimants, she had given up hopes of making dis-coveries, and she had contented herself with the use of a very capital umbrella which had cost her nothing.

"I see this very distinctly," said Mrs. Jumbold, musing; "Annis Greenwell, and probably she alone, can solve the mystery of the death of Richard Grover."

"I reckon so, too," threw in Mrs. Rhodes.

"And it is essential that she should be seen, questioned, and made to relate what took place."

"Oh, ma'am! for mercy's sake, let me not be brought into it."

"It is impossible for me to say whether you can be kept out of it. It is certain that the whole case must be put in the hands of the police, and it is a matter of felicitation to myself that Providence should have enabled me to unravel a mystery which the police were powerless to solve. I will take the umbrella with me, Mrs. Rhodes, of course. You will hear further, shortly, I have no doubt in the world. I wish you a very good afternoon."

But once before in her career had Mrs. Jumbold experienced happiness such as that which uplifted her now. That former occasion had been the discovery made by her in Whinbury Copse.

CHAPTER XI.

"I LOOK toward you, sir," said the York policeman, whose acquaintance we have already made.

"And I, sir, catches your eye," responded the Sowden policeman, with promptitude.

"This, sir, is the tenth anniversary of my union with Mrs. Physic. Ten years of matrimonial felicity have left me, not what I was once sir, no."

"Your wife's health, sir, and many of them."

"The children that have accrued to me since that union are awful to contemplate."

"Personally or numerically?" asked he of Sowden.

" A little of both, sir. My spouse has a knack of bringing twins into this world of woe, where units would prove more acceptable. Once we dreaded trins, sir, but it proved lusty male twins. So much for them numerically. Personally they are a caution — not, understand me, in their natural condition, but as modified by civilization. Most of my sons are boys, sir, and boys require attention at three points, the elbows, the seat, and the knees. Between the periods of my wife's confinements, which are annual, she lives in a state of patch. At one moment the knees are through, and by the time she has patched the knees there is a cleavage at the seat, and when the seat is mastered, the elbows break out. Would you believe it, sir, no sooner has she grappled with the elbows, and mended them, than the knees are at it again. Thus she spends her unconfined life, in revolving from knees to elbows, with the seat intermediate."

" It is shocking. I'm an unmarried man, I'm glad to say."

" Well, marriage is not to be enterprised, nor taken in hand, unadvisedly or lightly; for it leads to two necessary results which are alternative—doctors or babies. And a man before he marries must make up his mind as to which he prefers, or, more strictly speaking, which he abhors least, and make his choice accordingly."

" How do you mean ?"

" Let him take a sickly woman to be his partner, if partial to doctors ; but if his tastes lie in the way of babies, then let him look out for a female with a vigorous constitution."

" It is most unusual to drink a health in unfermented liquor," said the Sowden police-man, raising his cup of coffee to his lips ;

"but may I wish your life to be as agreeable as is this cup, with the coffee and the milk combined in harmonious proportions, and the sugar evenly sweetening both."

"Thank you, sir. You observe the unusuality of toasting in unfermented liquor. I regret to learn that you are beerbiferous. I am a teetotaller, otherwise I should have offered you spirituous beverages; but I do not on principle. Since the illustrious Duke of Clarence inaugurated self-immolation in liquor, the number of victims to drink has been truly appalling. It is now nine years and a half since I took the pledge, and I have kept it ever since. Had I been a teetotaller ten years ago, I might not now be a married man, and the father of one—two —three—four—five——"

"What are you counting on your fingers, Mr. Physic?"

"My children, sir. I can seldom keep them all in my head. One or two are constantly slipping out. Let me see, where was I last? Five, I think; that was Gorgianna. Six and seven in a lump."

" Lump, Mr. Physic?"

"I mean twins. Eight died in teething. Nine,—sharp lad that. Ten and eleven in a lump again. Twins I mean. Twelve, the present hurdygurdy. I have been for ten years constrained to dwell among those who are enemies unto peace, and all along of liquor. I was in liquor when I first saw the present Mrs. Physic, I was fresh when I proposed, and I was drunk when I married her."

Mr. Physic shook his head, the Sowden policeman shook his. Then each raised his cup to his mouth, and looked at one another over the rim, whilst drinking. The York officer withdrew his mouth from the wholesome, but not exciting beverage, for a moment, to sigh. The Sowden officer sighed responsively.

"And may I ask what has brought you here?" asked Mr. Physic, replacing his cup in the saucer.

"I'm after a lady," answered his friend.

"Not in a matrimonial way?" sympathetically.

"No, in a business line."

"And who may she please to be, sir?"

"A young lady who lives in the Minster yard. I'm not a going to nab her, you know. But I want to speak with her a bit, along of something."

"What young lady, if I may be so bold as to ask?"

"Miss Greenwell; her as lives along of Mrs. Furness."

"By ginger!" exclaimed Mr. Physic. And then, apologetically: "I teetotal my oaths, sir. I generally swears by treacle, but when I'm much decomposed or enraged, I rise to ginger, as pungenter. But I never overstep that limit. I said, By ginger! for you surprised me. I have had some acquaintance with that lady, along of that theft at Midgeroyd, in your neighbourhood."

" Indeed."

" I found a party who wore those articles that were stolen, sir, or some very like them ; and I went to the house in which the same party lived, and there I found Miss Greenwell, the party you're after; and the party I was after had hooked it. It was a rummy go."

" Did you make any inquiries of Miss Greenwell ?"

" Of course I did. You don't catch a weasel asleep, in an ordinary way, do you? But she knew nothing of it."

" What has become of the party who had the stolen articles ?"

" My party, as I said, has hooked it. When she——"

" She, a woman !"

" A woman, certainly. When she ascertained that I was coming, she made off, and has not since returned. This leads me to suppose that she was privy to the theft."

" And what had Miss Greenwell to do with her ?"

" Nothing at all. She went there to vist her on charity."

" And whilst visiting her the party made off."

" I suppose so."

" It almost looks as if Miss Greenwell must have been a party to her escape."

" If you mean to say that your party was a party to my party's hooking it, I cannot say that I agree with you."

"There are some coincidences which seem to need a clearing up, Mr. Physic."

"I quite agree with you. As I remarked on the occasion, of all rummy goes, I had met with none rummier, and I considered this as the ne plus ultra rummiest."

"Miss Greenwell comes from Sowden."

"Indeed, sir, I am glad to hear it."

"The theft took place in Sowden, or adjoining it."

"I am aware of that also, sir."

"And Miss Greenwell allows the party wearing the stolen articles to escape."

"It is remarkable also," said Mr. Physic, "that your party observed to me, in answer to close examination, that she had first observed my party on the very day after the burglary took place. Have you come to see your party relative to the same affair?"

"No, on quite another. But I think we

two might call together, and prosecute our inquiries conjointly."

" I am all agreeable, " replied Mr. Physic.

Annis was labouring through the voyage of La Perouse when the servant told her that there were two " gentlemen " wanted to see her.

" Who can they be ?" asked Miss Furness, looking up from her needlework.

" I think they're policemen, miss," replied the servant.

"Police ! what can they want with you ?"

Annis dropped her book and turned very pale. She had dreaded lest further inquiries should be made about the red-veiled woman, and had been for a couple of days in nervous apprehension of a visit of this kind. She feared interrogation, lest she should be forced to yield up the secret of who the wearer of the veil was. Now she saw clearly what Earnshaw had done. He had stolen the articles of female clothing he had used for his disguise. If her evidence led to his conviction for this offence, in all probability there would be drawn from her sufficient to bring against him the more serious charge of having caused Richard Grover's death.

She remained seated, with her hands on her lap, looking blankly before her.

Miss Furness ordered the servant to show the officers into the dining-room, and to tell them that Miss Greenwell would be with them directly.

"Now, Annis, dear," she said, "what is the matter?"

"Oh, Miss Furness, I wish you would come down with me, I am so afraid of those men."

The lady promised to accompany her, and then asked again what was the reason of the visit.

"Nothing concerning me, exactly," answered Annis; "but you shall hear. Only tell me first if I am bound to answer every question put to me?"

Miss Furness looked at her with surprise. What could the girl be so anxious about? She replied—

"Certainly not, unless put on your oath. But when you do speak, let it always be the truth."

"You may trust me," Annis said.

"Yes, dear, I know I may. Now, come along, and let us find out what these men want. You have quite perplexed me, I assure you."

They found the policemen examining the marvels of nature and curiosities of un-civilized art which adorned the room. With the origin of each Mr. Physic had been professing his acquaintance to his brother officer; and before the arrival of the ladies

he had been indulging the Sowden policeman with an account of swordfish, China-
men, nautili, and idolatry in general, according as his eyes rested on the thrusting
weapon of the fish, the hat and shoes of
the Celestial, sea shells, or images of Buddhist
deities.   It was difficult to light on a subject with which Mr. Physic was not fully
conversant.   The variety of objects in the
room gave ample scope for the exhibition of
his knowledge, delivered with gravity and
solemnity, in an undertone.

And then, just before the entry of the
ladies, he of York had poked him of Sowden
in the ribs, and said—

" You may take the word of John Physic
for one thing, sir.   He is a judge of female
beauty.   You can't mislead him in that.
He is a perfect connoisseur.   And he'll tell
you this—your party is a tip-top stunner."

The tip-top stunner was in a thick black

woollen gown, very neat and quiet, with white cuffs and a narrow white collar edged with black, a little silver cross suspended to her neck, her complexion beautifully clear, like a delicate camellia leaf, with the faintest tinge of colour in the cheeks. Generally it was lighted with the most glorious flush, like the afterglow of an autumn sun on snowy heights; but anxiety had moment-arily blanched her. Her profusion of burnished hair, braided and plaited behind her head, was the only colour about her. Her eyes were of a saddened depth, that they had lately acquired; they sank before the stare of the two officers, as they bowed stiffly and eyed her curiously, and regretting the interruption, expressed a hope that their intrusion would not be for long, but there was a little matter, &c.

"What is it?" asked Miss Furness. "Will you take a seat?"

"Thank you, ma'am," said the Sowden officer.

"Thank you, *miss*," said Mr. Physic, looking at his brother officer with indignation.

"There is not much to detain you, ladies," began the Sowden policeman; "but I have with me an umbrella, which is thought to belong to one of you. Is it yours, miss?" offering it to Miss Furness.

"No," answered Bessie, "I have not lost one. Do you own it, Annis?"

"May I look at it?" She took it in her hand, examined it carefully, and said, "Yes, this is certainly mine. I left it in Sowden."

"Do you remember where you lost it?" asked the country officer.

"No, I really cannot remember. I did not have it long, and I did not know that I had left it about anywhere."

"On what day did you come to York, miss?"

"She came on the morning of September 11th," replied Miss Furness.

"And it was found on the night of September 10th," said the man, looking fixedly at Annis. The girl lifted her eyes, startled, and met his eyes.

"Where did you find it?" she inquired.

"It was found in Sandy Pit Lane. Did you go there that night?"

"Yes, I did."

"There was an unfortunate little affair took place on the night of the 10th, and as you were on the spot where it happened, much about the time, it is thought that possibly you may be able to give some evidence which will clear up what is at present shrouded in uncertainty."

"What little affair was it?" asked Miss Furness

"Merely the death of a man under extraordinary circumstances," was the reply.

"Annis," said Miss Furness, "do you know anything about this?"

The girl hung her head, folded her hands, and made no answer.

"Of all the rummy goes," began Mr. Physic.

"Presently, if you please," said the Sowden officer, turning on his comrade and silencing him.

"It would be satisfactory if you would give us an answer," the policeman said.

Annis looked up, and said, in a scarcely audible voice, as she caught Miss Furness's arm for support—

"I should prefer not to give my evidence now. I can say something, but I will not, till put on my oath."

"Very well, miss," said the officer. "You

will come to Sowden to-day or to-morrow, please; this matter must be investigated."

"I will go there to-day," she answered; "that is, if Miss Furness will spare me."

"Yes, that will be best," said Bessie. "Get it over, dear, and be back as soon as possible."

"And now, please," said Mr. Physic, ill at ease at not having been brought into sufficient prominence in the foregoing conversation, "I should like to put a few questions, miss."

"I am ready," answered Annis.

"That was a regular conflustercating affair that, the other day, now wasn't it? And I taking you for the old lady, with you sitting in the dark! I'm gingered, but it was almost comical, and it must have dumbfoozled you a bit, miss, with me putting you through a cross-examination about what you knew nothing at all. Wasn't it, now?"

"I do not exactly know what to answer. What is your question?"

Miss Furness looked indignantly at Mr. Physic, and the Sowden policeman seemed provoked.

"Didn't I state my views about its being, of all rum goes, about the ne plus ultra rummiest?"

"I will trouble you to put proper and intelligible questions to Miss Greenwell, or to leave the room," said Miss Furness, haughtily; and then turning to the other officer, asked whether he could not put the inquiries instead of Mr. Physic.

"You be easy, miss," said the York functionary. "I'm coming to the point, right on end. Now, Miss Greenwell. About that woman. When did you see her first in York?"

"I told you the other day, the thirty-first of October."

"Can you be sure of this, Miss Green-well?" asked he from Sowden.

"Yes, I can," she answered. "I think I could swear to the day."

"Now, then," began again Mr. Physic, "I want to know, was the woman in the house when you called?"

"Yes, she was."

"Did you know she had stolen the articles? You'll excuse me for asking, miss. But professional duty requires it, and it's a painful obligation imposed on us officials, to discharge our duties at the expense of our personal feelings, and I may add, of our genteelness."

"I certainly did not."

"No, I did not suppose it for one moment. You will excuse my asking the question which implied a suspicion. You did not observe her destroy the veil, did you ?"

" No, I did not see her burn it."

" I should think not.   She was a vast deal too dodgy for that.   But though she might escape your observation, she couldn't evade my penetration.   And you had not been to her house before?   And only this time you visited her in charity, according to her wish ?"

" Yes, she asked me to go and see her, as she was in want."

" One moment, Mr. Physic," said the Sowden officer.   " Allow me to put a question to the lady.   Miss Greenwell, had you known this said party before?"

" Before what ?" nervously, evasively.

" Before that party came to York?"

Annis made no reply.

" Not likely; don't insult her, sir.   There are bounds which even professional exigencies

should not force a man to overstep," said
Mr. Physic, with stateliness, and a depre-
cating look at his comrade.

"Miss Greenwell," said the country officer, " do you reserve the answer to this, as
well as that to my former question ?"

" I do."

" I think, Mr. Physic, we need trouble
the ladies no longer."

" Certainly, certainly.   Ladies, a good
morning."

" You have promised, miss, to be at
Sowden this afternoon or evening.   There
is a train leaving York at 3·25, another at
4·20, a third at 6·50.   Probably you will
not go by a still later train.   I may rely on
your being in Sowden by to-morrow, may I
not ?"

" Yes, you may expect me."

" And where shall I find you, miss ?"

" At Mrs. Rhodes's, Kirkgate "

When the policemen were gone, Annis sank into a chair and covered her face. Miss Furness was surprised immeasurably by the questioning of the officers, and the answers of the girl. She could not in the least comprehend the drift of the latter part of the inquiry. That with reference to the death in Sandy Pit Lane explained itself.

" What is this all about ?"

" Oh, dear Miss Furness, do not ask me now ; it will all be cleared up shortly. Perhaps you will trust me when I tell you, in confidence, that one in whom I am thus far interested, that he is a great sufferer, and that he once rendered me a great service, is now in danger ; and that had I spoken I should have endangered his life. Even now, I shall, I know, have to speak what, if he does not escape, will bring him to the gallows."

CHAPTER XII.

SMALL idea had Hugh, as he sat joking with Laura in his uncle's drawing-room, that his little Annis, whilst he was thus engaged, was approaching Sowden.

The Arkwrights and the Doldrums saw a good deal of each other now. Hugh's accident had been the means of drawing them together, and a week rarely passed without an evening being spent by Mrs. and Miss Doldrums at Belview Cottage, where lived the millowner, or by Mr. and Mrs. Arkwright and Hugh, at Doldrums Lodge.

Laura had persuaded the young man to make of her a sort of confidante, or, more correctly speaking, she had burst in on his

confidences, and taken them by storm. On
the very first opportunity of speaking to
him in private, she had insisted on knowing
something, nay, everything about Annis,
and had not rested satisfied till she was
made acquainted with the leading circumstances of Hugh's "charming romance," as
she termed it. Having acquired the requisite information, and taken violent
possession of Hugh's secrets, she became his
most zealous champion. She would not
hear a word spoken in disparagement of him
or Annis, she upheld his right to make his
own choice, lauded his good sense in having
broken away from the usual run of engage-
ments, asserted her conviction that his
judgment was to be relied on, and proclaimed
her opinion, that so long as a girl was good
and true and honest, she was worthy of any
man. One forcible argument in favour of
Annis, Laura invariably fell back upon.

"You know, if it hadn't been for that blessed smoke-jack, I should have been a factory girl myself. People would not be shocked and scandalized if Hugh Arkwright were to propose to me; but the only difference between Annis Greenwell and myself is, that my father patented a smoke-jack, and hers didn't."

And then her mother would add: "It's quite true, my dear. We was only in a very small way, when Doldrums, who is now mouldering in his grave, with room beside him for me, and some inches over, discovered the patent smoke-jack, the contrivance of which is simple and yet marvellously efficacious, which has been extensively used and largely patronized, and which continues to give general satisfaction."

Hugh was not reluctant to make Laura to a certain extent, and within certain limits, a confidant. She was sympathetic, and of a kindly, affectionate disposition, which led him to trust her. He was glad to have some one to whom he could speak on the subject uppermost in his thoughts. It had become almost intolerable to his frank nature to have a matter concerning him most nearly tabooed at home. His uncle never alluded to the absent girl, and Mrs. Arkwright had been given a hint by her husband not to speak upon the past. Martha, he had few opportunities of seeing, and he shrank from seeking her out, lest he should cause his uncle annoyance. Mr. Furness was resolutely silent on the subject. Hugh saw a good deal of the vicar, and occasionally approached the topic, but Mr. Furness invariably turned the conversation.

Mrs. Jumbold, however, was ready at any moment to give him her mind on the "scandal," as she insisted on designating it to his face; but when she did, it was to throw out such odious insinuations as to the reason why the girl had been removed from Sowden, that Hugh would never allow her to speak on the subject.

But Laura was very different. Her heart overflowed with sympathy towards the young man in his solitude, and she used her best endeavours to relieve his desolation, by giving him the opportunity he desired of speaking about her, who was ever present in his thoughts, to one who could enter into his feelings. She made him describe the absent lassie to her, and listened to his glowing descriptions with pleasure that she took no pains to conceal.

"And then," was Hugh's usual conclusion, "Annis is so good."

"Ah, there! Goodness last of all."

"Not a bit. If she were other than good I could not love her."

"And pray how do you know she is so

excellent ? Have you had much opportunity of conversation with her ?"

" A woman carries her character on her face,—in her eyes," answered Hugh. " It is legibly written by Nature or Providence, I cannot say which, and he who chooses may read it."

" Indeed ! And is my character inscribed in my face ?" asked Laura.

" Distinctly."

" And so you judge of a woman's soul by her looks."

These confidences did Laura much good. They opened her eyes to the reverence and devotion that the true, honourable man feels for what is womanly in woman. It startled her to find that a man could so entirely penetrate through all the disguises which artifice puts on, that he could brush aside all that was acquired and irrelevant, and detect at once what was genuine and noble and pure. She began to realize that there were elements in woman's nature which exactly meet the cravings of man's nature, elements which are inherent, and which education does not always succeed in developing. She began involuntarily to contrast herself with the ideal woman, and to feel how false much that was in herself proved to be. Slowly she awoke to the consciousness that she herself was not true to her own nature, and that there were in her germs of good which had not been given room for expansion.

On the evening that Annis arrived in Sowden, Mrs. and Miss Doldrums had come to Belview Cottage to tea and supper. On similar occasions, and these occasions were, as has been already intimated, pretty frequent, Mr. Arkwright amused himself with the Relict of Jonathan Doldrums, making an occasional sally upon his wife, drawing her into the conversation, bewilder-

ing her, covering her with confusion, and
dismissing her with a laugh.   Laura's
mother in no way interested him, but he
bore with her company, and relieved the
load by making a fool of her, so as to give
Hugh opportunities of cultivating Laura's
society, and forgetting his past delusion.
Mr. Arkwright was convinced that his
nephew was slowly, yet surely, coming round
to his views.   He had not made an attempt
to find out where little Annis was hidden.
He had not spoken to him of her, and above
all, he displayed an unmistakable liking for
Miss Doldrums, and took no pains to conceal the pleasure he found in her society.
This, poor simple Hugh never thought of
doing.   The possibility of his breaking faith
with Annis did not for a moment enter his
head, and he scarcely considered whether
other people might form a different opinion.
It was talked of in Sowden, however, as pro-

bable that Hugh would think better of his engagement to the mill girl, and would eventually propose to Laura; and people generally thought that this was the best thing he could do. Miss Doldrums had a fortune, Annis had none; the former occupied a good position in the social world of Sowden, the latter held none. Advantages manifold would accrue from a marriage with Laura, but only disadvantage from a union with Annis. As for such trifles as honour, plighted troth, and disinterested love, public opinion took no account of them ; they were not palpable facts of monetary value.

Mr. Arkwright heard it whispered that Hugh and Laura were attached to one another, and he chuckled to himself, and gave no denial to the rumour. Mrs. Jumbold made it a text for expounding her views on the indifference to morality distinguishing the present generation from that to which she herself belonged. "For my part," said she, "I can't think how a young lady like Laura Doldrums (with her means), can associate with a young man of smurched character. I'm sure when I was young, if I had had a suitor whose morality was half as bad as that of Mr. Hugh Arkwright, I would not have tolerated his presence. I always thought Miss Doldrums a decent girl with some propriety—and she has a considerable income — but I suppose the old proverb is true, 'Birds of a feather flock together;' and if she is so ready to wink at the licence of her follower, her own character may be a little blown upon; there is no knowing."

Of course Mrs. Rhodes had also her little say on the matter; she took a different line. She thought Mr. Furness ought never to have huddled Annis out of the place; that it was like "them church folk, always to stick up for the rich and take no account of the poor." That if she had had her way, Annis should not have been allowed to go till Mr. Hugh had been brought to sign a paper, swearing that he would marry her, and that if he did not he would pay heavy damages.

"And now," said Mrs. Rhodes, "we'll have to go to law about it, and try our best to get brass out of him. But them lawyers will swallow half." To which John replied—

"Hold your tongue, missis. No one will be better pleased than I, if it turns out as folks say. I never thought well of them young folks getting together, and I shall be glad if they forget one another, and get suited according to their stations."

"And ain't you going to law, to get damages? They always do in a case of breach of promise of marriage. And big

damages they get sometimes, I've read i' t'
paper."

"Certainly not," answered John. "And
I will trouble you, missis, to hold your
tongue about this business; it is no concern
of yours."

But Martha felt troubled and disappointed. She had believed in Hugh. She
had promised to trust him fully, unre-
servedly, that day she waylaid him at the
stile; and she had conscientiously kept her
promise. She agreed with her father, that
if Hugh should prove unfaithful, no notice
should be taken of it; the young man would
be unworthy of a thought, unworthy of
Annis, and it would be a matter of rejoicing
to her to know that her cousin had not
fallen into the hands of one undeserving of
her. But her great, noble soul refused to
disbelieve in Hugh. She observed him at
the mill, she watched his face in church, and

felt comforted; it was the countenance of an
honourable man who would be true to his
word, and better still, true to that love
which, when real, is enduring.

One evening Martha slipped into the
vicarage, to consult Mr. Furness on the
point.

"My dear Martha," said the old man,
" do not trouble yourself. Leave all in
God's hands."

And she was comforted.

Martha, could not but believe in good,
and believing, have trust. However often
unworthy and mean motives were brought
before her, as influencing her mother and
sisters and friends, she put them from her,
and went forward in her confident silvery
course, unaffected by them. She saw what
was evil, but took no impression from it;
her own clear sense of right she supposed
must actuate others; and when their conduct

appeared to her opposed to such a sense, she
shut her eyes. Indeed, her life, like that
described in Talfourd's 'Ion,' flowed—

" From its mysterious urn a sacred stream,
   In whose calm depth the beautiful and pure
   Alone are mirror'd; which, though shapes of ill
   May hover round its surface, glides in light,
   And takes no shadow from them.

" You don't happen to have heard of the
convertible coffin, have you, Mrs. Doldrums ?" asked Mr. Arkwright after tea.

" No ; a coffin, and convertible !"

" Yes. I have ordered one for Mrs. Arkwright."

" Oh, Henry !" from the lady alluded to.
" What about coughing. I'm very well."

" It's the thing they put dead people into,
you know," said Mrs. Doldrums, with a con-
fidential nod.

" You have not seen the convertible
coffin, then ?"

" Certainly not. If I had, I'd sure to

have made a note of it; that's if my eyes
would have permitted. What is it like,
may I ask?"

"It is useful for various purposes. It
makes a very good bed. Also, inverted and
expanded, it serves as a dinner-table."

"A rather small one," observed Mrs.
Doldrums.

"Not so very small as you would think,
madam. The sides and ends are made to
lift up, like the leaf of a table, so that the
size is by that means doubled; and then
again it opens down the middle, and the lid
can be inserted, so as further to increase the
surface."

"I don't quite see how the shape would
permit," objected Mrs. Doldrums, all in
good faith, and exhibiting a profound interest in the subject.

"That can only be understood by personal inspection. But I have not done with

the convertible coffin yet. It makes a charming cradle for a child. Again, it is adapted to serve as a portmanteau. The sides are fitted up with pouches, to contain, on the one side, soiled linen, and on the other side, razors, lather-brush, strop, combs, and hair-brushes. Then the lid internally is crossed with red tape, for the insertion of collars, or note-paper and envelopes."

"And may I ask who are the patentees?"

"Hearse, Mould, and Company."

"Would you kindly write down the address. My eyes are not what they used to be, or I would not trouble you."

"Do you hear what nonsense my uncle is talking to your mother?" asked Hugh, aside to Laura.

"Yes," she replied. "He delights in making game of her, and she swallows all he says. To-morrow she will be insisting on my writing for one of these new coffins, and I shall have to pretend that I have done so."

"It is a curious hobby for an old lady to have," said Hugh.

"It is a very harmless one," answered Laura; "but it is tiresome at times, especially when she insists on being laid out, and gives full instructions how the funeral is to be arranged. She actually, one day, had the napkin put over her face, and taught me how to lift it, so as to show her features to any sorrowing friend who might wish to have a look before she was screwed down. Hark! Mr. Arkwright is at it again. Look how bewildered your aunt seems. Oh, Hugh!"

"Yes, Laura."

"I want to say something to you quite privately. I am afraid of speaking here, lest Mr. Arkwright should overhear me. Could you manage to show me the greenhouse?

What I have to say is something very particular and very private."

" Come along then.   There is a lamp in the conservatory, and the flowers — the camellias—are well deserving of inspection. My aunt is very fond of them, and Mr. Arkwright likes to use the greenhouse as a smoking-room."

A door led from the drawing-room into the conservatory, which was small, but in good order, and well stocked.   The care of this little place devolved on Mrs. Arkwright, and in it was spent all the spare time she could afford.   The flowers were not rare and expensive, but showy.   At the present time there was but little to enliven it except white and crimson camellias in great abundance, and rows of blue, pink, and white hyacinths, exhaling a delicious odour. In these hyacinths Mr. Arkwright took great pride.   He had a business acquaintance in

Hamburg, who supplied him annually with bulbs, and he pretended to be able to distinguish the varieties with the precision of a connoisseur.   A few pots of cyclamens and narcissuses completed the show.

The conservatory looked bright and cheerful, as it was snug and warm.   The floor was boarded, and covered with a felt carpet. There were two or three chairs inviting occupants, not garden chairs of dismal green painted wood, hard to sit upon, and with uncomfortable backs, but cushioned.   From the roof depended a lamp, which lighted the house sufficiently, and brought out the rich colours of the flowers.   The temperature was high; white linen screens drawn over the roof shut out the black night sky, prevented the upward radiation of the heat, and reflected downwards the light of the lamp. Only at the side facing the garden was the greenhouse open to the outer darkness.

"It is quite a snuggery," said Laura. "Our conservatory is three times as big, and not one quarter as comfortable or as pretty."

"Do you notice the supports and ribs?" asked Hugh: "They are coloured blue and red, and a painted cornice runs along the three walls. This little amount of colour has a wonderful effect in giving finish, and the carpet and chairs add their testimony to the comfort."

"So they do," said Laura. Then, with a little change in her face and an alteration in her tone, she asked, "Do you know what I have to say to you?"

"I have not the remotest conception," answered Hugh; "but I am sure it will be something agreeable, for whatever you say is pleasant to me."

"You flatterer!" she exclaimed, for an instant recurring to her former manner.

"Now, I assure you, I have something very particular to tell you of, which others—your uncle, for instance—know, but which I have no doubt is kept from you." She spoke earnestly, and with a tenderness in her manner such as she always assumed when speaking with Hugh on The Subject. The young man noticed this change, and divined at once that she was going to say something about Annis.

"What is it?" he asked, with roused interest.

"Do you know that either to-morrow or Monday your little friend will be in Sowden?"

The colour rose into Hugh's face, and his eyes sparkled with delight.

"Laura! is this true?"

"I have heard it. Indeed, circumstances have rendered it necessary that she should be sent for. Have you heard nothing of them?"

"Not a word.   No one except you speaks
to me of—of—HER."

"No, and they might refrain from telling
you this.   Be composed, Hugh, there is a
good fellow, and I will tell you all."

"Is it anything to distress me?"

"No, I think not.   But there is something odd and inexplicable in the matter,
which I do not understand."

"Tell me all about it."

"You remember how that a horrid fellow,
a man-monkey, or something of that sort,
was found dead last autumn in Sandy Pit
Lane."

"Yes, I remember the circumstances very
well.   A girl, Martha Rhodes, came to the
door here one night, to tell us that she had
found a corpse, and my uncle and I went at
once to the place where it lay.   It was that
of the converted gorilla.   It was a nasty
sight.   Why do you allude to this?"

" Was it not on the same night that Annis Greenwell left ?"

" Yes, it was so ; on September the eleventh."

" Well, it seems she was in the lane that night."

" That cannot have been. I saw her at the vicar's, and walked with her to the station."

" What, before you found the body ?"

" No, just after. I ran from home to Mr. Furness, to tell him of what had taken place, and found Annis in his room."

" She must have been there, however, for her umbrella was discovered near the spot where the corpse lay."

" Who found it ?"

" Mrs. Jumbold. It seems that she sallied forth, directly her husband was sent for, and went at once to the place, and there, at the side of the lane, lay the umbrella.

She said nothing about it at the time, lest the owner should take alarm, and not identify it; but she waited her opportunity, and, one day, Mrs. Rhodes seeing her with it, claimed the umbrella. Off went Mrs. Jumbold to the police, and I believe one has been sent in quest of Annis. The vicar told them where she was."

"This is very odd. Martha must have had the umbrella."

"No, she had not. Mrs. Jumbold taxed her with it being hers that same night, and she declared she had not brought one from home with her."

"You have not got the story quite correctly," said Hugh. "Mr. and Mrs. Jumbold were at tea at our house that evening, so that the surgeon was on the spot as soon as I was. I remember that his wife persisted in coming also, notwithstanding my aunt's remonstrances; and I remember her asking Martha, in a casual sort of way, whether she had an umbrella. I thought at the time it was an odd question for Mrs. Jumbold to put to the girl, but it passed out of my head. I have no doubt now that Martha had taken the umbrella with her, but had forgotten it in the alarm and flurry of the discovery."

"No, you do not know all. Mrs. Rhodes confesses to having sent Annis to meet Richard Grover in Sandy Pit Lane that night."

"You do not mean it? Did Annis go?"

"She did, supposing that you wanted to see her."

"I!"

"Yes, Mrs. Rhodes sent her out, having led her to believe that you wished to say good-bye to her."

Hugh paced up and down the conservatory in the greatest agitation.

"Poor little lamb!" he muttered, and almost sobbed.

"But I met her directly after, at the vicarage," he said, abruptly stopping, and recovering himself. "I cannot understand this. The whole thing is a puzzle to me. She had come by no harm; she was pale and agitated when I saw her, but that was all; and she certainly knew nothing of Grover's death, for she cried out with horror when I mentioned it to the vicar. It will all come right."

"It will all come right, certainly," said Laura.

Then Hugh went up to her, and took her hand between his.

"Thank you, you good, kind girl; thank you for telling me this. I had rather have heard it from you than from any one. All this has been kept from me, as if I were not of all people the most interested in it. Promise me one thing, Laura."

" Yes, anything, almost," frankly, and looking up with a bright smile into his face.

" When Annis comes, will you see her, and be kind to her ?"

" She shall come and stay at our house. She must not go to the Rhodes's, after the vile way in which the woman there behaved to her."

" Thank you, Laura."

" And I will do all I can to make her happy and comfortable; and "—in a low voice, accompanied by a twinkle in the eyes—" I will talk to her about you, and tell her how true you have been, and of the many chats we have had together about her. Will that satisfy you ?"

He pressed her hand, and lifted it to his lips.

When he raised his head, his eyes fell on the surface of glass commanding the front garden.

There, looking in on him, was a face.
A face once seen in the combing-shed, once
again in the train, now, for the third time,
and always by the light of flame. Once at
the time of that awful flood, once before
that plunge into the black canal, now—
what did it signify?

There it was, scarlet and purple, with the
glittering white teeth, with the nose flattened
against the glass, the thick patches of eye-
brow, the seams and warts horribly distinct;
with the great glaring dark eyes fixed on
him—the whole standing sharply out of a
blue-black night.

"Good God!" Hugh gasped.

"What is it?" asked Laura, startled by
his tone, and by the expression of his face.

"He is not dead, after all."

Laura followed the direction of his eyes,
and saw nothing. The face had disappeared
into the night.

CHAPTER XIII.

WHEN Annis arrived at the Sowden station, no one was there to meet her. She had not expected any one, for she had not told the policeman by what train she would come. Yet it struck her with a sense of loneliness when she left the station, that on returning to the place which, after all, was home to her, though all that really constituted home was gone from it, she should find no one on the platform to take her hand, and greet her with words of kindness and welcome. She gave the little portmanteau Miss Furness had lent her to the care of the porter, promising to send for it, and then she left the station.

During the journey she had considered

what was best to be done, and had resolved on going at once to her old cottage, where she expected to find Joe concealed, and warning him to escape, as her evidence must be given on the morrow, and then search for him would ensue as a certainty.

She took the way by the river, which, she expected, would be the least frequented, and met no one.

A few stars were shining, and by their light she was able to see her path. They were reflected in the sluggish river. A gaunt skeleton of a barge, which had been washed up on the bank at the flood, and had gone to decay out of its element, was the only novel feature on the well-remembered way. The old familiar sights and sounds were there; the ruddy light beyond the hill over Halifax, the pulsating reflections of the iron furnace, the rows of illuminated windows of a cloth mill running all

night, the fretting of the river over the
weir, the noises of the railway, the evening
bell of Sowden Church.

The wind was chilly, blowing down the
narrow valley, and tracking the course of
the water. She had a knitted shawl round
her, crossed over her chest, and tied by the
hands of Miss Furness behind her back, and
over that a black silk mantilla, which
flapped, with the harsh sound silk always
makes, in the cold rushing air. She had a
pair of black woollen gloves on: she was
glad of them. She did not wear a bonnet,
but a black straw hat, and she had no veil,
so her face was very cold. Glad was she
when she heard the babbling of the beck
which flowed into the river, and trod the
plank bridge over it, and stepped over a
stile, and saw against the grey sky the outline of the sand rock, and the gable of the
cottage in which she had spent so many

quiet happy years. Often of old had she
come briskly along this path towards it,
singing and rattling her little dinner can,
with the ends of her red handkerchief, or
grey shawl, flying behind her, as she
quickened her pace on seeing the saffron
glow from the window of the kitchen
parlour, that she might meet her mother,
and sit down to a comfortable tea by the
ruddy fire.   But now those days were over
for ever.   The little red flapping kerchief
had been given away, and with it had gone
the blithe dancing heart.   The mother was
departed from earth, the windows were all
dark, and the hearth was cold and black.

The girl sighed, and tears formed in her
eyes, but she was too anxious and frightened
to allow her thoughts to rest long upon the
past.

"Oh, if Joe is not here!" she said to
herself, with sinking heart.

Joe was not there, apparently.

Annis went to the front door, and tapped lightly. The shutters of the window were up, and she could not see into the room. Then she passed round to the back door, and tried that; it was fast. The little low window of the kitchen behind had no shutters: she looked in, but could see nothing but blackness. As she touched the glass, leaning against it, in her attempt to see, the lower portion moved. Surprised at this, she put her fingers to the bar, and without difficulty succeeded in throwing up the sash.

She pondered over this. How was it that the window was not hasped? It was impossible that it could have been forgotten when the house was locked up. She drew the sash down again, and ran her fingers along the junction between the movable lower sash and the upper one, which was stationary. Then she guessed how it was that the window was unhasped.

It was possible to thrust a knife-blade through the crevice, and with it to press back the hasp, and so allow the sash to be thrown up.

She at once guessed that Joe had been there. He had told her that he could enter the house without a key. As certain as that he had been there, was it that he was out at the present moment, for were he within he would most surely have fastened the window. Although it was possible for one on the outside to turn back the hasp, it was of course impossible to fasten it again.

But there was other evidence that Earnshaw had been there, for out of the gloom appeared a little white creature, which leaped on the window sill, and plaintively mewed. It was the watchman's favourite cat.

Annis stood moving the window up and down, uncertain what to do. She could enter the cottage if she chose, but she hesitated to do this. The thought came upon her, that if within, Joe could come to her, and there would be no possibility of escape ; and, though desirous of saving him from danger, she was fearful of him. She felt in her pocket for a pencil and a scrap of paper, intending to write a few words as well as she could in the dark, but though she had Martha's last note with her, with its blank leaf, she had no pencil. The bitter wind made her shiver.

"Oh! I wish I knew what to do," she said, faintly.

"Annis."

She heard her name spoken in the soft musical note of a woman, and yet she knew that the speaker was a man.

"Joe," she whispered. whilst her whole

frightened little body quivered. "Joe, is that you?"

He glided towards her : he was still in woman's apparel, as she could see indistinctly by the starlight.

"What have you come here for?" he asked, in a low tone. "Have you come to see HIM?" and his voice quivered with suppressed rage.

"No, no, Joe," she answered, putting up her hands appealingly. "I have come here to save you."

"To save me," he said sweetly. "Me ! So you still think of ME. Come to save ME."

"Indeed I have," feebly, and yet vehemently, notwithstanding the weakness of the voice and faintness of the little spirit that urged her to speak. "Joe, the police have found out about my having been with the man-monkey before — before — you know what."

" Well."

" And I have to appear before a magistrate to-morrow, and be put on my oath, and make a statement of what I saw."

" Well."

" Oh! I cannot tell a lie. I must say that I saw you, and then you will have the police after you. I cannot tell a lie, if they ask me what took place."

" No," said the man, " you cannot. You would not be the little true Annis I have known and loved so——"

" Oh, stop, stop !" in terror.

" And what am I to do ?"

" Joe, you must make your escape at once ; the police will be after you to-morrow, not before."

" You will not have to go before a magistrate till Monday, you may be quite sure," said Earnshaw.

" Then you will have two whole days."

He gave a short harsh laugh.

" They will be on my track to-night."

" No they will not, they know nothing as yet."

" There is something else to make them hunt me down."

" What ?   The veil ?"

" And something besides."

" Do not tell me what it is," she begged in her fear; " but fly at once, and in your present disguise."

" I have been seen.   Before an hour is over, the police will know that I am in Sowden."

" You have been seen, Joe ?" echoed the girl.   " Who by ?"

" By HIM."

" What, by Hugh !"

" Yes.   He saw me.   Shall I tell you what I was doing, dear lassie ?   I was on the look-out to learn something of him for you—and for myself. God ! I thought the fellow was dead !"

" Why, Joe ?"

" Never mind, but I did. And I saw him, not half an hour ago. A fine faithful lover, Annis !" He burst forth into his loud booming tones, in his scorn.

" Oh, hush, hush !"

" Shall I tell you how I saw him ?"

She clasped her hands over her bosom, on the little brooch of jet and Cornish diamonds, and looked up with a white, imploring face. But it was too dark for that to be seen.

" I saw that true-love of yours speaking tender things to a lady, looking into her face, and she with her eyes lifted to his, and her hand clasped in his hands, just as I once saw him and you in this house. And I saw him bend over her and kiss her pretty fingers. Ha ! a true lover that, a faithful lover that! I hate him more than ever for his forgetfulness of little Annis."

A faint quivering sigh, half sob, broke from her heaving bosom.

" And as he lifted up his face, he saw me," continued Earnshaw.

" Joe !" She spoke in a mournful voice. " Is it true."

" Is what true ?"

" What you told me of Hugh—of Mr. Arkwright ?"

" I swear by G— it is perfectly true. Did I ever tell *you* a lie ?"

Again she sighed heavily ; and then after a moment of struggle with herself, in the same sad voice she asked—

" Now what are you going to do ?"

" I am as safe here as anywhere. I cannot hide amongst a crowd, as do other men. My face will not let me."

"Joe, has no one seen you here except Mr. Hugh Arkwright ?"

"No one."

"I will go and speak to him."

"That you shall not," said Earnshaw, fiercely, catching her by the arm.

"Let me go," she said, calmly. "I will only ask him not to mention having seen you."

The man did not speak for nearly five minutes, but walked up and down the back of the house, never, however, taking his eye off Annis, who stood cowering against the wall, with her hands over her eyes, and her heart beating wildly. In the bitterness of her suffering she forgot Earnshaw, and thought only of Hugh, unfaithful, and herself, deserted and miserable. Now she understood why Martha had not mentioned Hugh in her letters. Annis longed to throw herself into the arms of her cousin, and bury her head in a bosom which she knew was true, and there sob out her griefs. Earnshaw stepped up to her, whilst she was thus thinking, and said, with his hands holding her wrists, and drawing her palms from her face—

"Go, go and beg him to spare me. Plead with him for *Me*. Ah, ha! That will be charming. You will find him with his new love hanging on his arm, and you can tell him how you feel for ME."

"I will go," answered Annis, recovering her calmness, and speaking in a constrained voice. "Yes, I will go. Where shall I find them—him, I mean?"

"In his uncle's house. You must be quick, if you would catch them together. And then, Annis, when you have heard what he says, and know what my fate is to be, and when you have seen him and his new deary together, then come to Me."

" Why ?"

" Come and tell me whether I am to fly at once, or not ; come and tell me. Come and see me once more. Hark !"

Far away and faintly chimed Sowden church clock.

" That is nine o'clock. Before long they will be parting,—kissing and squeezing hands. Ha! you understand me. Go and see it all, and then speak to him. And at eleven o'clock come to me. Not here. No, it will be too late for you to come here. You will find me in Arkwright's mill-fold. You will find me at the mill door."

" It will be so late," said Annis.

" But do you not want to save Me ?"

" Yes, indeed I do."

" Then you will do that. Avoid the watchman, but he will most likely be at one of the other mills. At the stroke of eleven come to the door that you used to go in at day by day. If you cannot be there at that moment, I will be within; then tap thrice at the door."

"How can you get in, Joe?"

"I went off with the keys. Now, away with you!"

She turned and left him, with her heart as dark and sad within as the night without. She glided through the garden into the lane, then went to the bridge, and there she stood still, and leaning her hands on the rail, bent her head upon them and wept convulsively.

She remembered when that little bridge had been swept away, and when she had clung to the breast of one who had borne her through the swollen beck, and had felt his arms embrace her, and her own little heart glow with a strange rapture. Half a year had passed, and what events had taken place in those few months! Her mother gone, the whole course of her life altered, her heart a prey to emotions she had not known before, her mind open to ideas she had not previously dreamt of.

When she had recovered herself, she hurried up the lane, wiping her eyes, and steeling her heart for the approaching interview.

She felt her blood curdle as she passed the spot where the death of Richard Grover had taken place. She reached the branch in the lane, turned towards the Arkwrights' house, saw the light in the windows, and the illuminated conservatory, and stood still. How was she to manage to speak in private with Hugh? She did not like to go to the door and ask Sarah Anne to tell him that she was there, and wished to see him. She shrank from the smirk and knowing looks of the girl, and she knew that such a visit would become the subject of gossip all over the village directly, and its impropriety would be freely commented on. No, it would be better to trust to an accident.

She opened the garden gate and glided through; then, stepping off the gravel walk on to the turf, crept towards the conservatory. She looked at the beautiful flowers and the brilliant light with her dim forlorn eyes. There was no one within, but she could faintly catch the voices in the parlour, as the door communicating with the drawing-room had been left half open by Hugh when he and Laura returned to the company.

Annis stood and shivered outside, chilled without, and weary and bruised in spirit. She heard music from the inner room, a piano being played and a female voice singing, and she wondered whether that voice belonged to her who had supplanted her. She looked up at the stars with a longing to be with her mother beyond them.

" Leave it in God's hands," the vicar

had said. But oh, how terrible was the result!

She could not endure the cold much longer. She turned the handle of the green-house door, and found that it was not fastened. She opened it a very little way, and the warm air rushed out on her. What if she went in? She would rather see Mr. or Mrs. Arkwright than the servant, for they would not mention her visit, and would probably allow her to speak to Hugh for one minute. Still hesitating, she thrust the door further open, and now the cold wind leaped in, swept through the conservatory, and slammed the drawing-room door.

" Ach!" exclaimed Mrs. Arkwright, look-ing up from her game of whist. " Du lieber, Hugh. Will you have the goodness. That naughty greenhouse door is open, I am sure. Did you hear the shocking bang. Go shut it, dear fellow."

And so Hugh almost immediately went to Annis.

Without the least suspicion that she was there, he sprang from his chair, laid down his cards, opened the door into the conservatory, and entering, saw, standing on the garden steps, a little black-draped figure, with a face of deadly pallor, out of which two large dark eyes shone with a subdued light.

He recognized her in a moment, shut the door behind him hastily, and started forward.

She came in now, leaving the step.

"I want to speak to you one moment, Mr. Arkwright," she said, in a calm, unnatural tone.

"Annis, dear, dear Annis!" He had her hands in his instantly. They were as cold as stone, and did not return his pressure; but he scarcely observed it.

" You dearest little girl," he said, devouring her with his beaming eyes. " How ill you look; have you been unwell?"

" I have been very well, thank you."

" I must have a kiss."

She repulsed him, turning her face aside, whilst a sudden twinge of pain contracted the muscles of her mouth.

" What is the matter, my own?"

" I am not yours, Mr. Hugh."

" Annis!"

" I have come to speak about something else," she said, constrainedly. " Will you listen to me for a moment?"

" You will drive me mad," he exclaimed. " What does this mean?"

" I want you to do me a great favour," she said, and then, with her voice softening, " in consideration of old times. You saw some one a little while ago—Joe Earnshaw."

" I did," with a puzzled look.

" Will you promise me to tell no one you have seen him ?"

" Annis, what do you mean ?"

" For the sake of old days passed away for ever," she went on, in a mournful tone, " I want you to do this one thing. You have ruined my happiness, make this amends. It is not much."

" I will promise anything you like," answered Hugh. " But I cannot understand you, Annis. Why are you so cold with me ? Have you ceased to love me ?"

She looked up at him. Her great brown eyes began to fill, a tremor ran over her face, and a flame kindled in her cheeks.

" Let me go, let me go !" she wailed, struggling from his grasp.

" Annis !"

She was gone.

He stood motionless, bewildered, gazing

at the night through the garden door. His heart stood still.

"She is no more mine—no more mine!" he repeated. "My God, my God! this is terrible. Anything but this!"

Then he heard his aunt calling him from the drawing-room. He shut and bolted the conservatory entrance, and returned in a numbed condition of mind to the room he had so lately left, and reseated himself at the table.

"My dear fellow!" exclaimed Gretchen, impatiently. "How shocking you play! Freilich! I had rather a dummy as you."

"He is preoccupied," said Mr. Arkwright, with a wink at his wife, and then at Mrs. Doldrums, and finally a sly glance out of the corners of his eyes at Laura.

"Excuse me, aunt; I am not fit to take a hand to-night. I have a good deal on my mind."

"And heart too," said Mr. Arkwright. "Ahem, we understand."

Hugh looked dreamily at him, and then tried to collect his thoughts sufficiently to go on with the game, but in vain.

"We will excuse you," said his uncle.

He threw down his cards and left the table.

CHAPTER XIV.

"Mrs. Doldrums' carriage is at the door," announced Sarah Anne.

"Oh, dear!" Laura said. "I should have preferred walking."

"And then Hugh would have accompanied you home," put in Mr. Arkwright, slyly.

"I have no doubt that he would," replied Laura at once; "he is always ready to be civil and obliging."

"I will at all events see you to the gate," said the young man; and as he took Laura to the carriage, he whispered, "I have seen Annis."

"When?"

"This evening; but only for a moment. All is not quite right, I fear."

"Oh, stuff! Lovers are always full of fancies."

"I wish it may be only fancy," Hugh said, despondently.

"I will seek her out to-morrow, and insist on her coming to the Lodge," Laura said. "Good-night, Hugh."

"Good-night, and many thanks, Laura."

The carriage rolled away, leaving Mr. Arkwright and his nephew at the garden gate.

"Come and have a· pipe and a glass of brandy and water in the greenhouse," said the former, turning towards the house.

"I will join you there presently," answered Hugh. "I want to run into the town first."

"It is rather late."

"I will be back directly."

"You will find me in the conservatory; don't be long."

Hugh passed into the lane. His uncle looked after him with a grim smile, and said, when he was out of hearing, "We have you fast now, young fellow."

Hugh went at once to Kirkgate, and knocked at the door of the Rhodes's establishment. The shop was closed, but there was a light through the glass over the door, which showed that the family had not gone to bed. The poor fellow could not rest without an explanation from Annis. Her behaviour had maddened him. What had she meant by saying that she was no longer his, and by her intercession for Earnshaw? A temptation to connect these two facts together presented itself before him, but he turned from it in sickly horror. Annis and that awful watchman—the pure, simple maiden, and that murderously intentioned maniac — what could be the connection between them? He knew the hateful creature's passion for the girl, and he was now made aware of her interest in him. And she could be no more Hugh's little Annis! Good God! Did she mean that she belonged to another? He recoiled from the thought.

"I will not think of this," he said.

The door was opened to him, after he had been kept waiting some little while, by Susan, holding a candle.

"Lor, Mr. Hugh! who ever would ha' thought it were you?"

"Who's there?" called Mrs. Rhodes, shrilly, from the back room.

"Susie," said Hugh, "tell me, please, is Annis with you?"

"Annis!" The girl stared at him, and then laughed. "Nay, she's not here. Whatever put that in your head, sir?"

"Are you certain?"

"Ay, I'm as sure as I'm standing here."

"Where is Martha? I must see Martha immediately."

"Martha," called Susan, "there's a gentleman at t' door, seeking thee, lass."

"What's all this about?" cried Mrs. Rhodes, without leaving what she was engaged upon.

"It's somebody wants me, mother," said Martha, going into the shop.

She was as much surprised as her sister to see Hugh at the door; she was distressed to observe his anxious expression. She went to him at once, without asking questions, and telling Susan not to fasten the bolt, as she would be back directly, she stepped out into the street with him.

"Thank you, Martha," he said. "Now tell me, where is Annis."

"I do not know."

"I have seen her to-night, and have

spoken to her, so she is somewhere in Sowden."

"You have seen our Annis!" echoed Martha, standing still in astonishment, and looking at him. "We thought it likely she would be sent for soon; that she might be coming, happen, to-morrow, or maybe Monday, but not to-night."

"She is actually here."

"And you do not know where to find her?"

"No, I do not. I thought she would be with you."

"I could have made sure she'd ha' come first to me," said Martha, with a slight tone of disappointment in her voice; "but happen she thought otherwise."

"Where can she be?"

"I think it likely enough she is at the vicarage. If she didn't come first to me, it was because she wanted to see Mr. Furness before others. And she may have felt a sort o' shyness o' meeting mother after what has taken place. Yes, I reckon that is it," with some confidence. "She went to the vicarage, and is staying there. You may set your mind at rest. I feel sure that is what has happened. We shall see her, dear lass, to-morrow. I'll get back as soon as ever I can fro' my work."

"This is not all I have to say," pursued Hugh. "Annis is so changed."

"Ah! I thought she would be. She'll be a right lady now."

"That she always was," said the young man, with a sigh; "but she is altered in another way. She spoke to me so coldly and indifferently, as though I were a mere acquaintance."

"You wouldn't have her jump into your arms, now," said Martha, in her blunt, off-hand manner.

"No. But she seemed not to care a bit to see me, not to be in the least glad to meet me, after all these months of severance."

"She was shy. Do you think she'd ha' come to see you, if she hadn't cared for you."

"She came to ask a favour of me, quite concerned about a third person, and in a formal manner. I am afraid all is not going on smoothly. Martha, you must find out for me what is at the bottom of this."

"Psh!" said the girl; "I've no patience with you. Annis is all right. You should know her better than to mistrust her."

"She told me distinctly that she was no longer mine."

"Then she didn't mean it. She was silly. Maybe she is a bit jealous. Some folks love to make mischief, and they may have been telling her spiteful tales."

"They must have been tales of pure invention," said Hugh, simply.

"Oh, there are a deal o' tales about, along of you and Laura Doldrums."

Hugh stood still and laughed. "Is that all?" he exclaimed. "*You* never suspected anything, Martha, did you?"

"I trusted you," the girl replied.

"Now I must be going back. As you are so satisfied that Annis is at the vicarage, and that her manner towards me is the result of a misunderstanding, I shall rest more content. I was in a thorough fidget before I saw you. Poor little Annis! I cannot endure the thought of a cloud coming between us, if only for a few hours. Good-night, Martha."

And he went, with lightened heart, towards home. Martha returned, to find herself in a hornets' nest. Her mother, Rachel, and Susan, were all prepared and waiting to attack her.

"Here's pretty goings on!" exclaimed Mrs. Rhodes, the instant the girl came in. "So much for your chu'ch ways. May we

never have the like o' them i' our sect.
And what is more, lass, I won't have my
house treated like this. What does yond
fellow mean by axing if we'd Annis here?
What is he after, coming here this time o'
neet? Look at t' clock, lass; it's nigh on
eleven. I know what folks will be saying
if they see young men come rapping at my
doors at this time o' neet, and thy father
safe and snoring i' bed half an hour agone."

"Eh! I wouldn't be a go-between,"
sneered Rachel. "It ain't I as would lower
myself to that. It wouldn't strive all I
could to make a leddy o' yond lass, and have
her lookin' down on us, and shamed on us
all as are her relations."

"Martha," threw in Susan, "so thou
knows where Annis is a hiding. And
thou'rt boune to bring her here for
Hugh Arkwright to be sweethearting
her."

"I'll have none o' that i' t' house," protested Mrs. Rhodes. "If Annis is boune to come here, as I suppose she must, there being no other place for her to go into, I'll look sharp after her, and not have her trailing after all t' lads i' t' place."

"Mother," said Martha, with perfect composure, "I believe that Annis would not think of coming here."

"No, I reckon not. We ain't grand enew for her fancy," sneered Rachel.

"There's many a slip 'twixt cup and lip," said Susan; "and if what folks says is true, Hugh Arkwright ain't a going to make a fool of hissen by marrying Annis, as thou'rt so chuff over."

"No," Mrs Rhodes exclaimed, in her harsh voice, with a toss of her head, "she won't demean hersen to come to her poor relations now. But when she's found out gentlefolks ain't going to make so much o'

her as she thinks for, then she'll come sneak-
ing here to be taken in, you'lt see !"

"Mother," said Martha, without showing
the least symptoms of being put out of
temper, "I think you have quite mistaken
the dear lass."

"I mistake her! That's like enough,
you saucy young minx. It's you is ever
over right, and me is ever wrong."

"I beg your pardon, mother. I did not
mean that. I think you've mista'en
Annis's motives in not coming here."

"Pray, what motives are they?" contemptuously asked Rachel, tossing away the
piece of sewing she had been engaged upon.

"I think, mother, she'd not like to come
here after what you did to her."

"What *I* did!"

"I don't mean to offend you, mother;
but you know she mightn't feel over comfortable here, thinking of how you'd deceived

her, and sent her out to the man-monkey, pretending it were Hugh as wanted her."

Martha spoke with great simplicity and quietness, but the words had their effect. Her mother darted at her a glance of fury, but was silenced.

" And what mucky hoile (hole) dost think she's gone to now ?" asked Susan.

" I think, lass, t' vicar has ta'en her in for t' neet."

" The vicar !" exclaimed Rachel.

" Well," laughed Susan, " happen t' vicar ain't much better nor us."

" Halloo there !" called a loud voice from the top of the stairs. " You womenkind, ain't you going to stop them clappers ? How can I go to sleep if you're fratching half t' neet through ? Shut up, will you, or I'll leather-strap you all round."

It was the voice of John Rhodes from bed : it silenced the women.

CHAPTER XV.

As Hugh entered his uncle's house the clock of Sowden church steeple struck eleven.

He found his uncle in the conservatory, with his pipe in his mouth, lounging in his easy chair, beside a table, on which stood spirits, and a small jug of cold, and another of hot water, reading his newspaper.

The lights in the drawing-room had been extinguished. The suspended lamp in the greenhouse was low, so that Mr. Arkwright read with difficulty.

"Just in time," he said; "I can't make out this smudgy print any longer. There is no more spirit in the lamp, and it is going out."

"Shall I fetch you the moderator from the drawing-room?"

"Never mind. We can talk; we don't want light for that, I suppose, and obscurity will help to veil your blushes. The lamp won't go out altogether for another half, hour, but give a sort of twilight glow, suitable for romance, eh!"

Hugh did not understand what his uncle meant, so he answered indifferently: "If you do not want light, I am sure I do not. My cigar-end yields sufficient for me." He drew his chair round, so that the back might be against the garden front. He remembered the horrible vision of the face glaring in upon him from the outer darkness, and, rather to avoid the reminiscence, than expecting a recurrence of the circumstance, he moved the seat so as to face the camellias.

"Dismal night," he said: "wind piercingly cold."

"But there is plenty of warmth within," with a nod of the head towards Hugh.

"It is a pity the gas is not brought along this lane, so that we might not have the trouble of lamps," Hugh observed.

"Oh!" said his uncle, "it is you who are changing the topic."

"We were on no particular subject, that I am aware of."

"No, but approaching one by slow degrees."

"What topic?"

"Well, I suppose I must dash at once *in medias res*. I congratulate you heartily, my dear boy."

"You congratulate me!" exclaimed Hugh. "What on earth is the subject of congratulation?"

"Sly fellow.   Do you think I do not know?"

"I am at a loss to comprehend your meaning."

"What a long *tête-à-tête* you had in this place, Hugh."

"Yes, I had something very particular to say to Miss Doldrums."

"And you kept us waiting for our game of whist in the most unconscionable manner; but we were not disposed to interrupt you.   And she is quite agreeable, I suppose?"

"She is very agreeable," said Hugh, on whom his uncle's meaning dawned.   He was provoked, but at the same time amused. He drew a long whiff of tobacco, and blew it leisurely out, with his eyes on the crimson camellia.

"Uncle, I never saw a plant so full of flower as that.   It is beautiful."

"Changing the topic again, Hugh! Sly dog."

"What is the native country of the camellia? Do you know, sir?"

"Timbuctoo. Hang your camellia! We are talking of Laura."

"I did not mention her."

"No, but you were thinking of her."

"She was far from my thoughts, which were then on the camellia."

"Laura, be that the subject of our conversation."

"Then, uncle, I shall go to bed."

"Fudge, boy. I know your heart is full. Talk to me."

"My dear sir, you are entirely mistaken if you think I take an extraordinary interest in Laura. I like her very much; indeed, I am fond of her, as a sister, but no more."

"You don't mean to tell me," began Mr. Arkwright, incredulously, "that all those *tête-à-têtes* mean nothing. What were you chattering together in. this snuggery for, this evening, unless you liked her more than a sister? Didn't you pop the question this evening? You had a glorious opportunity."

"Certainly not."

"Then you were a monstrous fool. You had the best possible chance. A bright, pretty winter garden. Flowers all round, air warm, hyacinths smelling, glass glittering—it was just the very time and scene for a romantic young fellow like you. Don't let it slip next time."

"I have no intention whatever of proposing to Miss Doldrums."

"Then why are you trifling with her affections? She is fond of you, is always talking of you, praising you, running after you. I should say, she was madly in love with you. And you encourage her, and draw her on. You are bound in honour to make her an offer."

"Bound in honour I am to do no such thing," said Hugh, with temper.

"Gammon. I guess what you refer to. That is all over."

Hugh turned sharply on his uncle. Did he know anything which was concealed from him, anything which would sever Annis from him for ever.

"Why over?" He asked.

"Because—on my word," burst forth the manufacturer, starting up, "you are enough to make a man swear. I never do such a thing—I should be sorry to begin the practice. But I would give five shillings to be able to say, Damn you. I believe an oath is an escape provided by nature for the feelings when brought to high pressure. Upon my word!" he added, relapsing into his chair; "I think I never came across such a confounded fool in all my life."

"Uncle, I will not stand this."

"I am addressing the Turk's head on the bowl of my pipe."

Mr. Arkwright and Hugh smoked on in silence, drawing hasty whiffs, and puffing the smoke out in little compact clouds.

"Shall we return to the consideration of the gas?" asked Hugh, at last.

"No, decidedly not!" very angrily spoken in answer.

"Then I will finish this cigar and go to my room."

"Hugh! none of this nonsense. You must marry Laura."

"I shall certainly not. In the first place, she would not have me, and in the second, I am otherwise engaged."

"Not have you! She'd jump at you."

"Then she is not the person who would suit me."

"No; none suit you but little sniggering——"

"Uncle, stop." He spoke firmly.

"Hugh. You do not mean to tell me that you persist in that absurd romance of last autumn! This is intolerable. I did not think such a jackass—I am alluding to the Turk's head, Hugh, don't go. Hugh, give up this folly, and be rational."

"I am quite in my senses."

"No you are not. Common sense points out Laura as the very girl who would best suit you. She is nicely educated, is full of spirit, fun, and good nature, is universally popular, has lovely hair and eyes, and a charming expression, and to crown it all, is immensely rich; and all to be had for the asking. Hugh, do you hear?—to be had for the mere asking. Here am I toiling and moiling to make a few hundreds, and there are thousands to be had for the mere asking—the mere asking! You have but to hold up your little finger and the money is yours. By George! I wish bigamy were legal, and I would try to get Laura for myself. It is tempting Providence, to throw away such a chance. So much gold lying at your feet, and you will not stoop to pick it up. So many thousands extended to you, and you will not stretch out your hand to grasp them! You nincompoop!—Turk's head, I address you!"

"Would it not be as well, uncle, if you were to take a cigar, and allow me to pitch that pipe away? It is likely to produce a quarrel."

Mr. Arkwright paid no attention to this suggestion.

"Boy," he said, taking the pipe out of his mouth, and leaning his hand which held it on the table. "Listen to me."

"I am attention, sir, but please to address me in future, and not the Turk's head."

"I have reckoned on your proposing to Laura Doldrums, and my hopes and expectations have been built on the prospect of your marrying her, and becoming possessed of her property. I must tell you that my affairs are by no means as prosperous as you might have supposed. I have had serious losses. The failure of the Leeds and Manchester bank clipped my wings a trifle. That rascal Armitage—you know—who bolted to America, lost me a couple of thousand pounds, not a penny of which am I likely to recover. Business has been slack, and I cannot dispose of the goods I have in stock. My yarns, made for the German market, to German weights, will not sell in England, and they encumber the warehouse. The machinery wants

renewing, and I have not the money in
hand to order fresh.   As long as this
German war lasts—and there seems to be no
prospect of its terminating in a hurry—I am
in a losing condition.   The flood did me
damage to the tune of some hundreds; and
I must have some prospect of money or I
shall go to pieces.   If you take Laura, you
can sink money in the business, and we shall
weather the storm and do well.   What I
want now is a few thousand pounds.   With
that I shall be able to hold on till the
tightness   is   past,   and   afterwards,   the
business   may   be   extended,   and   I   see   my
way to turning over a great deal of money.
You must please to remember, Mr. Hugh,
that you have nothing whatever of your
own, and that your future entirely depends
on your turning your present opportunities
to the best account.   You are in a fair way
to making a fortune now, if you will only

realize the rare chances put in your way, and use them effectually. You are in a business which bids to be prosperous, you are beginning to understand it. There is a certainty of money sunk in it quadrupling itself in a few years, if we can only tide over the present crisis. A series of untoward events have affected the concern at present—the failure of banks, the fraud of Armitage, the Continental war, and the imperfection and wearing out of the machinery. You may ask, why I do not borrow. Because I never borrow if I can avoid it. I shall have to borrow at a heavy rate, and I care not to burden myself further. I have a loan already, which ought to have been paid off, encumbering me, and one I would have relieved myself of this year, but for this deuced German war. No. What I want is a partner who can sink money in the concern. You are the

proper person to become my partner, and
the opportunity of obtaining the requisite
sum is open to you.   For the asking, you
may have enough to set me once more on
my feet, and give the concern a push which
will carry it on into success.   If you are
obstinate, pigheaded—I allude to the Turk's
head — I shall pass you over, and take
another into partnership.   I have had an
offer already, and I shall close with it
unless you yield.   Let me tell you, Mr.
Hugh, it is pleasanter to be partner than
clerk.   You wouldn't be particularly pleased
to see young Jumbold put over your head,
and you to remain as salaried understrapper,
eh?   Of course I should personally prefer
having my own nephew in the business
with me, to a young man who is no
relation; but the proposal has been made by
his father, who is ready to pay handsomely
for the partnership, and I shall close with

the offer if you do not accede to my wishes, and become a wise man, and a rich one into the bargain."

"I am sorry to disappoint you," said Hugh calmly; "but I adhere to my determination. I am bound to do so as a man of honour. When I asked Annis to be mine, I encouraged her to form an attachment for me, and I should be wrong if I disregarded her happiness in the pursuit of my own selfish advantage. A girl's feelings are too sacred to be trifled with. I believe the poor little thing loves me. If I ignored her feelings, and deceived her confidence, I might ruin her peace of mind, and cloud a beautiful spirit with distrust, and harden a green and tender heart to stone. I should outrage my own convictions. I am satisfied that Annis is the one woman best suited to me in the world. I love her, I trust her, I believe implicitly in her goodness, I am sure of her devotion to myself. I have borne much already for her, which has daily endeared her more to me, and she has suffered much for me. On my account she has been driven from her home, associates, and work, and has had to hide an aching heart, and bear the desolation of her bereavement, among strangers. She has been worried and insulted, and made the subject of gossip and scandal, because of me. I have already lifted her into a position of observation, and I cannot fling her back into oblivion. How can I calculate on the effect on her of such treatment as you recommend? And how do you think I could bear the humiliation of loss of self-respect, and consciousness that by all honourable men I was regarded as an infamous, perjured scoundrel."

"Confound you!" exclaimed Mr. Arkwright passionately; for now his blood was fairly up. "Do you mean to insinuate that ·I am not an honourable man?"

"Uncle," answered Hugh, who had worked himself into irritation by his long speech, "I am satisfied, that what you recommend to me, in the case of another you would regard as dirty, dastardly conduct."

"No such thing," said the manufacturer, angrily. "No man with any sense in his head would do other than approve of what I advise. If a man puts his foot into a wrong box, he will get out of it at once, with a consciousness that he is in a false situation, that is, if he is wise. If he is an infernal idiot, he will put the other leg in too, and proceed to lie down in his box. No reasonable man, I say, would think, that because you had been spoony once on a time on a little snivelling mill girl"——

Hugh bounded out of his chair, and in doing so knocked over the table.

" There you go with your damned precipitation! (You have made me swear, observe.)
This is in keeping with all you do. You
will plunge into a much worse mess than
this with just as little thought. Gad! this
water is hot enough that you have splashed
over my knee, but that water you want to
take a dip in yourself is a deuced deal hotter,
let me tell you. Pick up the spirit bottle,
Hugh. Look out for broken glass. You
have smashed both tumblers. Confound
the lamp! I wish it were not so near
out. Turn it up, Hugh, and let us see
where the fragments are : I don't want to
get my feet cut with glass. You have
boots on, but I only my slippers. What
a jackass — I am addressing my Turk's
head."

" Uncle !"

Hugh was standing where he had risen, his
back was towards the garden front of the con-

servatory ; facing him was the wall, trellised
over with creepers, not now in bloom, before
which, on a raised bed, were the camellias.
As the lamp had failed, the rich carnation
and white flowers had faded into the dusk.
A single spot of flame remained, and by its
light the white blossoms were faintly distinguishable, but the crimson flowers were
not to be discerned from the leaves.   But
now, as Hugh stood, flushed and angry,
with his eyes levelled at the gloomy bushes,
the flowers gradually detached themselves
from the darkness, and gathered distinct-
ness, then colour.   The white wax-like
blossoms lost their pallor, and flushed, the
crimson ones grew scarlet.   Hugh looking,
and not immediately observing, his mind
being preoccupied, saw his shadow flung
back and distorted on the creeper-covered
wall.   Then he started and turned, and
turning, saw his uncle risen, and his face

illumined with a coloured light, and his eyes
dilated.

"Good God!" exclaimed Hugh, "The
mill!"

CHAPTER XVI.

THE wind rushed along the vale, laden with
sleet. Black vapours with ragged outline
spread over the heavens, extinguishing star
after star. The night seemed to be a great
void of blackness, through which raced a
blinding scud of frozen particles, that struck
against every opposing surface, and on it
built little walls and ridges of watery ice.
A sickly nebulous haze clung about every
gas-lamp. Deserted causeways were crusted
over with dissolving sleet; whitening roads
were welted with black ruts; clogged bushes
shivered and shook off the ice lodging on

their twigs; windows were pattered on softly; leaves tingled, spouts gurgled, eaves dripped; Nature, oppressed with darkness and desolation, paled and blackened again, shuddering. An engine uttered far away a long protracted wail. A man slunk from the cold into a low public-house near the station, and shut the door behind him on the darkness and sleet.

A quaking girl ascended the steps of Arkwright's mill, her black dress patched with the outshakings of the cloud, that clung to her, and sucked the warmth from her, and feasted thereon, and dissolved into water drops. Then a hand, thrust out of the darkness, grasped her wrist, then hinges creaked, she was drawn within, and the door was shut behind her, and black as it was without, she became aware that there was a blackness blacker still; and that if there was a horror of being without, there was a horror more horrible still of being locked within.

All this took place as the Sowden steeple clock struck eleven.

The impervious darkness, the consciousness of being in it with one whom she dreaded, was unendurable to Annis. She bore it for a minute only. Her fears rose like a flood, and rushed over her. She would have fainted if she had not spoken. Her nervous system could not have endured the agony of terror longer by a moment without giving way.

" Joe, show a light, or I shall die," she moaned.

" Go up to the spinning room," he answered gently, in his thrilling musical tones, full now of a strangely sad pathos. " Go to the old reel, poor little lass, and wait. You will find light there."

" I cannot see," she whispered. There

was a tightening at her throat, as though she were strangling. "I cannot endure this darkness any longer."

"Feel your way. Shall I assist you?"

"No!" with a sharp cry.

She started from the door. That stone stair she knew full well. Often had she tramped up and down it with light heart or with sad heart, with buoyant spirits or with wistful longings, but never before with the stunned sensation in her brain, or the contraction of heart that she felt now, as with her hand against the greasy wall she groped her way up the oil-steeped steps. The man followed behind. When she considered that he was drawing nearer, the thought goaded her on. The old familiar scent of the foul oil that impregnated everything met her once more; the woodwork she knew was saturated with it, the very stone distilled drops of it, the iron was polished with it, the wool clogged with it, the window glass blurred with it. And with the scent of rancid oil was also an all-pervading subtle odour of gas.

When she reached the door of the spinning room she thrust it open with her hand, and went in. The light spoken of by Earnshaw was very faint; it was only that cast through the windows from without by the lamp above the gate into the mill-yard; this made a sort of yellow dusk within, especially towards the extremity of the long room.

"Go in there and wait for me," said Earnshaw.

"Joe, the gas is turned on, and is escaping," Annis said, as the hiss of the vapour and its nauseous scent met her on entering. "How is this? They generally turn it off at night."

"I suppose it is left on," he answered.

" Wait here whilst I go down." He turned and left her.

Annis remained in the great machine-encumbered room. The mechanism was quiet now. The great straps did not rush along the roof, setting numberless wheels in motion. The floor did not quiver with the vibration of the countless movements in the delicately - constructed machines. But all was not quite still. Throughout the room sounded the pfiff of gas apparently escaping from every burner.

Annis heard the descending steps of Earnshaw, then his tread on the basement floor, slow, heavy, distinct.

She listened, anxious for his return, as she was in a hurry to be off. If detained much longer she would find a difficulty in getting shelter for the night. To the vicarage she had purposed going, according to Miss Furness's direction, and in her pocket was a note from that lady to her brother, asking him to give the girl a bed for a night or two, and promising to come to Sowden by an early train on Monday. Annis, waiting and wearying, crept down the room towards the end which was partially illumined by the lamp outside. As she went along, on all sides of her sounded the gas, and the air became more heavily charged with it. She could scarcely breathe. She put her hand to the taps and turned them. This occupied her, and diverted her mind from Earnshaw. Tap after tap was open. She went down one side, feeling her way and groping for the burners, then up the other side, doing the same. And as she passed the windows she threw open some of the casements.

It was strange that the gas should have been left on. Usually each tap was shut off before the main was closed. This could not have been done on the present occasion when work was over. The gas must have been prematurely turned off at the main, and then let on again for some special purpose, and the unclosed cocks in the spinning room forgotten.

But this explanation was far from satisfactory.

Annis heard the tramp of the ex-watchman on the stair, then the sound of his feet entering the drying room.

She was wearied of waiting. She stood listlessly gazing out of one of the blurred windows into the darkness.

What seemed a fuming torch, rushed by with a rumble, and a star changed hue over the railway bridge. In reality, she saw the illumined steam of the engine of a goods train, and the shifting signal-lamp. Presently a leaky joint of a pipe in the room began to fizz and splutter, and a whiff of white steam to blow out of it. Then a drum high up against the wall trundled slowly, playing with the loose flapping belt.

Annis was surprised, perplexed, and alarmed. The steam had been turned on; wherefore, and by whom?

Then slowly up the steps from the drying room, and across the landing to the door of the long spinning room, came Earnshaw.

"Where are you, Annis?" he asked, standing in the entrance.

"I am here, near the reel," replied the girl. "You have been very long, Joe. I want to get away."

"I can speak to you now."

"Well, Joe, I wish you had let me say my say first. I have little to tell you, except that Mr. Hugh Arkwright has promised me not to mention to any one that he saw you. You are, in consequence, tolerably safe. Do make your escape at once; do, Joe!"

" Annis, it is impossible."

" I am sure it is not. You have two to three days clear for getting away."

" Annis, do you see me ?"

" Yes, why have you taken off your disguise ?"

He was in his waistcoat and shirt-sleeves. A broad-brimmed felt hat overshadowed his face. He was just distinguishable by the feeble glimmer through the window.

" I have thrown off disguise because it avails me no more. Escape is impossible."

" Not so ; make the attempt."

" I will make no further attempts. Annis, you have seen my face."

She did not speak, but shrank away, and putting her hand on the reel, turned it, looking fixedly out of the window.

" Can a man with a face such as mine disappear in a crowd ? I tried the disguise of female attire, wearing a veil over my face continually. That disguise is known, and avails me no more. The York police have discovered it."

" Oh, no," put in Annis, earnestly. " You forget they have not discovered who the red-veiled woman was."

" Not yet, perhaps, but before Monday it will be known. Do you think the Sowden and York officers will not enter into communication with one another? If they do, all will be found out. Poor little girl, you do not know everything that has taken place."

" Do not tell me !" she pleaded.

" Yes, you shall know all. I killed Richard Grover."

" Oh, I know that. I made sure of that; but you did not intend it, Joe, it was an accident. You were protecting me."

" I killed him purposely."

" No, Joe, no !" she cried, thrilling with horror.

"I had been waiting my opportunity for years. I found it at last, and I killed him. Richard Grover was the man who mutilated my features. He it was who disfigured and mangled my face, and made me an object of loathing to my fellow-men. He it was who blighted my life, who poisoned my happiness, who ruined me, body and mind, physically and morally. He it was who drove me from my home, drove me into seclusion, drove me to the maddening misery of being cut off for ever from the joys of life. Worse, ten thousand times worse, Annis! he severed *us*."

Annis sobbed, shuddering, shrinking against the wall, cowering before him, as his voice rose and rolled through the deserted room in loud booming tones.

"Little girl, I have loved you, oh, madly! Madly is indeed the right word, for my love has been the love of despair,

and it has driven me to do that which in
olden days I would have hated myself for
doing. But that I killed Richard, I rejoice,
I thank heaven. I would not have caused
his death, though, had he not insulted you.
No. I would only have beaten and
mashed his face with the slag on the road-
side, till it was reduced to a state like mine.
But I killed him—murdered him, if you
prefer the word—because he dared to lay
his cursed fingers on You."

" Let me go !" pleaded, in mournful tones,
the frightened girl.

" No, Annis, no ! I have not done my
history. You have not yet heard all. I
hated Hugh Arkwright."

Her heart gave a great leap, and then
stood still. She dropped her hands, and her
whole body became rigid.

"I hated Hugh Arkwright because he
dared to love you ; more than that, because

he won your love. You still cling to him, do you not?"

She did not speak.

"I will have an answer. Do you love him, or do you not?"

"Oh, indeed, indeed I do! You asked me this once before, and I answered you then."

"Yes, I knew it. I hated him for having stolen your affections. I would have none love you but myself, and if you could not return my passion, I would prevent any one else from assuming a right over you. I attacked Hugh, intending to kill him. I cut at him with my knife——"

A shrill cry of inexpressible anguish escaped from the girl; and she caught at the casement and held to it with both hands, fearing lest she should fall.

"I stabbed him, and plunged with him into the canal. I thought I had killed him,

but his fortune has been better than mine.
May be "—and he ground his teeth with rage
—"those prayers of yours saved him.   Ah !
if you had prayed for me, as you did for him,
I should have had more luck, and he would
now be rotting at the canal bottom."

She relaxed her grasp of the window, and
made a dart for the door.   Earnshaw caught
her, laughing wildly.

"Little one, do not try to escape.   You
cannot leave this place.   I have broken the
key in the lock, and there is no more egress."

She staggered back to her window, and
grappled it again, in a stupor of despair.

"Annis, you have not heard my story
out.   When I emerged from the canal, I
hastened to your old cottage ; there I lurked
till deep on into the night.   At last I came
forth, and I robbed the cottage of Widow
Lupton.   Not that I wanted money.   No, I
wanted a dress for disguise.   Having ob-

tained that, I sought you out. I had discovered your address. Tell me now, am I likely to escape? Is there the remotest possibility of a man, disfigured and conspicuous as I am, avoiding capture, when the police are on his track, thoroughly aroused, knowing him to be a murderer, a burglar, and a would-be assassin? No, Annis, no, I cannot get away. Were I taken, I should be hung, or, worse still, thrown into a mad-house, to rage my life out away from you. Whether I die on the gallows, or whether I am locked into an asylum, I care not. In either case I should not be with you, and you would be at the mercy of Hugh Arkwright."

He burst into a demoniacal laugh, loud, gulping, hideous, continued in echoing peals, as the hyena may laugh in the desolate places and empty sepulchres of the east, over the bones of a benighted traveller, who

has died of horror at the glare of the moon-
like eyes looking down on him, lusting for
his blood.

Then away he rushed towards the revolving drum, and about it he placed the
leathern belt, and tightened it around a
lesser cylinder; and running along the line
of motionless machinery, he touched a lever
here, turned a tap on, adjusted a strap there,
and directly, the rush of the wheels, the
whirr of the bobbins, the rumble of the
cylinders began. The mechanism was set in
motion throughout the room.

And Annis, clinging to the window bar,
in a dream, looked out on the blank wall on
the opposite side of the fold, a high wall
unrelieved by openings, belonging to the
warehouse of the adjoining mill, and saw on
the blank surface squares of lurid red, like
illumined windows over which were drawn
scarlet blinds; became slowly aware of an

intense heat, and a smell of burning, and a thickening smoke—but these her senses perceived, without conveying their impressions to her brain.

Then suddenly Earnshaw came up to her, his eyes glittering with red reflections, the light cast back by the wall irradiating his horrible face, his black hair bristling, his white teeth flashing, his hands extended towards her, and laying them heavily on her feeble wrists, he said—

"Annis, I have fired the mill. We shall die together."

She did not speak; she looked at him with unconsciousness in her dulled eyes, without repugnance, without appeal for mercy.

"Annis," he continued, speaking loud, to be heard above the rush and rattle of the machinery, but with a voice so full of volume that it would have been distinguish-

able in the midst of a thunder crash;
"Annis, dear, dear Annis! I swore that
no one should have you for his own. See
how I keep my word. I will not be torn
from you. We shall perish together."

The heat became more intense, the floors
were slippery with the exuded oil that
burst from every pore in little bubbling
springs. A pungent white smoke arose
from between the planks; a flickering blue
flame, like a Jack o'lanthorn, ran along the
floor, then stood still and changed hue to
pale yellow, gathered size and luminous
power, and shot up, a quivering tongue of
light. Drops ran down the walls, or fell
from the ceiling, as the heat dissolved the oil.
It was as though the horror of death had
fallen on the old factory, and it sweated in
its agony.

Now, without, appeared yellow walls and
gleaming window glass. A bare elder tree

in a corner became a tree of gold, the fold ground was brilliantly lighted with orange stripes, and in the light were seen black moving figures with illumined faces. Mill whistles shrieked, buzzers roared, bells jangled, and the gathering people shouted. Annis saw and heard, but neither spoke nor stirred. Earnshaw laughed over his handiwork.

The room was ghastly in the yellow light that smote in through the dingy windows. In the weird glare from the spout of flame near the further end, that stood up like a dancing cobra to the piping of a charmer, wavering and curling, rolling back and falling, and leaping up once more with lofty crest, the racing belts and rushing wheels were revealed, as they laboured at a profitless work. Phosphoric gleams flashed about, at a few inches above the floor, in an irregular, tentative manner, as though invisible hands were engaged in carrying flame from spot to spot. Then, all at once, the oleaginous vapour ignited with an explosion in several places, and began to gnaw at the heated boards.

A pipe burst with noise in the fire-consumed lower story, and the steam rushed out in a volume, screaming. The flaming oil swam over the floor, igniting wood wherever it came in contact with it. There were timber supports to the beams of the roof, and the fire corroded their bases. The heat was that of a furnace. Annis stood still at the open casement, looking out in the stupor of her terror.

All at once a glimmer of life stole through her dim eyes; she stretched out her hands and tried to speak, her lips moved, but no sound issued from them. She had seen Hugh in the crowd below.

CHAPTER XVII.

THE scene from without was wildly mag-
nificent.

The first story glowed like a furnace.
The flame had not burst through the windows, but consumed the interior; the light
began to appear, faint at first, gradually
intensifying in the second story, and cast a
yellow glare through the windows of the
long spinning room.

On the further side of the entrance-door
and stairs communicating with the rooms,
the flames had burst through the roof and
spouted into the air, to be caught by the
wind and borne away in flapping streamers

of amber and scarlet. Here the fire raged
with greatest fury, as it broke from the
drying room, which was full of hot wool,
that blazed at once, and, flying about in
ignited masses, spread the conflagration.
When the fire came in contact with copper,
the flames turned green. Sparks and
flaming particles rushed up at the over-
hanging clouds, as though labouring to
ignite them, and then fell away and went
out.

The sleet had stopped; only a few stray
spangling flakes rambled about in the glare
of the burning mill. The boiling vapours
which obscured the stars, reflected the light,
becoming lurid, as clouds of floating, glowing
copper.

The long window of the engine-house,
reaching nearly the whole height of the
factory, crossed within by landings of stone,
was illuminated, and the shadow of the huge

engine in motion, leaping up, then sinking, starting up again, and again falling, was cast on the panes.

The great gates of the mill-fold were closed and fastened, to keep the crowd from the premises. All the women, and as many of the men as could be persuaded to go, were cleared out of the yard. The alarums of all the mills in the valley within sight pealed continuously, but no engine had as yet arrived. The fire was momentarily gaining strength.

" By Gad!" said one of the men in the yard, " there's two i' t' miln. Dost tha see 'em, Wilfred ?"

" Ay, lad; I sees 'em."

The shadow of Earnshaw, as he rushed about the spinning room, crossed the lighted windows in succession. Annis remained at one little open casement.

" This is some confounded incendiary

work," said Mr. Arkwright. "What the deuce is the reason of it, I should like to know. Open the main door. Where is the watchman?"

"Here I am, sir."

"You have my keys. Get that door open."

"Uncle, the mill is on fire at three points. This is not the result of accident," said Hugh, coming up.

"Accident!" echoed the manufacturer, turning sharply round on him. "Look there!" He pointed to the second story windows.

Hugh looked. A chill came over him as he observed the little figure standing at the casement. The face he could not discern, as the strong light in the background threw it into obscurity.

"Can't open the door," said John Rhodes, hurrying up. "The lock is hampered. So is most o' t'locks."

" Burst the door open," ordered Mr. Ark-wright.

Hugh rushed off for a ladder.

" Come here, Fawcett," he called, to one of the men who worked for his uncle. " Help me. We must rescue those people in the mill, whoever they may be."

" Eh! let 'em burn," answered Fawcett. " It suited 'em to set t' miln afire, and they mun take t' consequences."

However, he accompanied the young man.

" Tha'll find t' stee (ladder) ower short, I reckon," said the man, with stolid composure. " I say, master, did ya ever hear t' tale o' t' fire i' one o' them big hotels i' Leeds ?"

" Oh, never mind the story now," said Hugh, impatiently, as he laboured to un-hook the ladder from the wall.

" Nay, it's a pity to do wi'out it; we

shan't get this done a minute sooner. There
was two men i' a room at top o' t' house,"
continued the imperturbable Yorkshireman,
"and when there was a cry o' fire, they nip
out o' bed, and grabble after their trousers.
And tha sees, it were dark, and they were
dazed like, and they got hold on t' same
pair o' breeches. And t' one man claps his
right leg into one leg o' t' trousers, and
t'other man he got his right leg thrussen
into t'other leg o' t' same pair, and he war
looking t' wrong road, so he'd t' seat right
afore him."

"Have you got that unhooked?" asked
Hugh.

"Bime by," answered Fawcett. "Well,
so they started off down stairs, yoked together by t' pair o' breeches, one pulling one
way, and t'other pulling t'other; and in
their fright and confusion away they go,
tumble-jumble from top to t' bottom, and

out into t' street fast by their legs. Now,
master, this is loose."

"Up with that end of the ladder on your
shoulder."

Fawcett obeyed, and proceeded to follow
Hugh, who supported the further end.

"I say!" called the man, a minute after.

"Well, what?" asked Hugh, turning his
head.

"Did ya ever hear t' tale o' t' robbers and
t' apit (bee-hive)?"

"No, and I do not want it now."

"Because the way we're hugging t' stee
reminds me of t' tale."

Fawcett proceeded to relate an anecdote,
but it was lost on Hugh, whose attention
was otherwise engaged. The man finished
it, as Hugh planted the ladder.

At this moment a flame, which had been
hurling itself against one of the windows of
the lower story, shivered the glass, and

shooting through, ran up the wall, licking it, as a serpent lubricates the victim it is about to swallow. By this, Hugh saw the face that looked out from above, and two little hands held towards him supplicatingly. He set his teeth.

" Give me an axe," he called.

" Here, sir," shouted the engineer.

"I say, I've a better tale by half than that o' t' robbers and t' apit. It's a tale about an oud woman and her bairn and a beer (bear). But I won't detain thee now. I'll tell thee when tha comes down," said Fawcett ; " and," he added, "if thee dos'nt brussen thy sides wi' laughing, I shall be capped." Then to the engineer : " I say, Wilfred, dost tha know t' tale o' t' oud woman and t' beer ?"

" Ay, lad," answered the man he addressed, "tha'st toud it me mony a time. Now clap thy foit (foot) on t' stee bottom."

"I'm doing so, Wilfred. Gearge, dost thou know?"

"Know what, Bill?"

"Why t' tale o' t' oud woman and t' beer."

"Nay, I cannot say I mind it."

"Weel, tak' hold theere along wi' me, and I'll tell thee. Hast thee gotten fast?"

"Ay."

"Weel, there was a man and wife had gotten a baby, as war laid i' a rocking cradle. They were no but poor folks, tha sees, so they hadn't much o' a cottage. No but a house wi' a chamber ower. And they got up into t' chamber by a stee. One day there came a grizzly beer in at t' door. It had escaped from a menagerie, happen. That I cannot say for sure. Choose how he gotten loose, he gotten theere. He came right in at front door, standing on his hind legs, and looking about him in a pined sort o' way. Weel, t' man, he were so flayed, he ran right up t' stee ; and he'd heard beers was mighty climbing beasts, so he pulled t' stee up after him."

" And where were t' wife and bairn ?" asked George.

" Nay, he never gave them a thowt; he were ower flayed for hissen."

Whilst this story was in progress, Hugh, axe in hand, was climbing the ladder. It was too short. It did not reach the window sill. He kept his eyes raised, fixed on the little face that looked down on him from above, lit by the rushing fire blast from a side window of the lower story.

By this time a beam had been brought to bear on the main door ; it was rested on the stone platform at the head of the steps leading to it, and was driven with violence against the black, iron-studded valves.

" Gearge ! thou arn't listening," said Fawcett, reproachfully.

" Eh, but I am !"

" Weel, then. In came t' beer, and made straight at t' bairn i' t' cradle. T' woman hugged up t' poker, and stood afore it. ' Gie him a crack ower t' ead, lass,' hollered t' man through t' hoile in t' floor above. ' Doan't thee lose heart. Mash his head for him, lass !' So t' wife gave t' beer a smart blow, and down he fell. ' Won't thee come doun and help to finish him ?' asked t' woman. ' Nay, lass, he might get up again. Gie him another crack. Bang him about t' ribs. Empty t' copper ower his head.' ' He's dead,' said t' wife. ' Art thee quite sure ?' asked t' man, through t' hoile. ' Ay. He's dead for certain.' ' Cut off his tail, lass.' She took t' chopper and did so. ' He's safe enew,' said her husband. " Now, lass, I'll come doun.' "

Hugh found the ladder far too short. The sill of the window overhung ; and, standing on the topmost available rung, he could only touch it with his hands.   Descending a step or two, he turned his head and called to the men below—

" Lift the ladder.   Put it on your shoulders."

" That reminds me——" began Faw-cett.

" Never mind what it reminds you of," burst in his comrade.   " Heave up t' stee, as t' lad bade thee."

" Don't tha see I'm about it ?" retorted the story-teller.   " Sithere, lad.   I'll take t' eend o' t' stee on my shoulders, and tha mun steady it, Gearge."

" Ay, I'll do that."

" And while I'm houding t' stee, I'll tell thee summut."

" If tha'st got wind to do't; but I'm jealous tha 'asn't."

Between them they elevated the ladder.

Hugh ran his hands along the wall, steadying it as it was raised.

"I say, Mr. Hugh!" shouted Fawcett, "Hast thou seen them monkeys in red coits and blew breeches on a stick, they sell at fairs? Happen thou'rt like situated now. Only don't thee go tummling over, like them monkeys."

"Gie ower wi' thy funning," expostulated George.

"I might as well let t' stee fall," retorted Fawcett.

Hugh's hands grasped the sill. The ladder was tall, and necessarily wavered as it was being elevated by the men, but he held it in balance. Now, close above him was the well-known, well-loved face, with its soft eyes beaming down on him, and the lips trembling with emotion.

"Annis, give me your hand."

She put forth her arm, and Hugh clasped her fingers.

"Can you support me? Are you strong enough?"

She put the other hand to his. He set the axe-haft between his teeth, clutched a stanchion, heaved himself up, and stood in the window.

The opening was too small to admit him, but holding to the stanchion, he used his axe to good effect, smiting at the window-frame, and breaking in the glass and lead-work. Those below shouted, but he cared nothing for their applause. Those working the beam for battering in the door rested for one moment, and then recommenced their work.

When Hugh had made a sufficient opening he stepped through, sprang to the floor, and caught Annis in his arms.

"My darling, my own darling!" he exclaimed. She could not speak. Her heart was full to overflowing, but the deep, earnest eyes told him how she loved him still.

"My dearest," he said, "we have no time to lose. Come to the staircase. We cannot descend by the window; that is impracticable with such a short ladder."

He led her towards the entrance.

Crash went the battering pole against the door, and the whole interior echoed at the stroke.

They came out on the landing.

A fierce howl rang in their ears. Earnshaw was half-way down. The stone flight leading to the first story ended in a platform of wood, movable, for convenience in hoisting bales of wool. Above this the stair was stone again. The landing of the second story was wood also. Earnshaw, at the first sound of the ram against the main door, had descended the steps and fired the lower landing.

Looking down, they seemed to be gazing into a well of fire. Volumes of flame rushed out of the door of the drying room, bearing with them a blazing snow of ignited wool, which whirled up and around, and sank, as eddies of wind were formed by the draught that rushed in from all quarters.

The platform of wood below them was a waving lake of flame. At intervals the planks warped and burst, with little reports, from the nails that had retained them. Then the rafters cracked. The heated blast, driving against the gas-pipe that communicated with the upper rooms, exploded it. The timbers of the roof overhead were scorched and glowing in places. A spiral column of lambent blue flame, transparent as glass, rose, tremulous and graceful, in the air, detaching itself from the body of flame, and ascended to the roof, where it spread out into a cloud of translucid nebulous fire, and in a moment yellow spots, then puffs of flame, appeared in the midst of it, and it vanished, leaving the rafters in a blaze.

From below, with his hideous face rendered doubly awful in the scarlet glare, looking up, uttering howls of frenzied rage, came leaping through flame, over fallen burning wood, the man who had caused the conflagration.

"You here!" he yelled at Hugh, plunging up at him.

"Yes, I am here," answered the young man, pressing Annis behind him.

He had left his hatchet in the window. He drew back into the spinning room, and shut the door.

Earnshaw cast himself with all his might against it, but Hugh kept it closed. There was a spinning jenny close to the door. He planted one foot against a projecting piece

of the machinery, and laid his back against
the door.

The madman raged behind him, beating
at the panels with his fists, then thrusting
his knife through between the interstices.

Hugh hoped every moment to hear the
front door give way before the blows of the
battering ram.

Earnshaw flung himself again with all his
weight against the door. Hugh could barely
hold his position. The iron against which
his foot rested gave way. Then he saw
the floor sink, bending beneath the weight
of the jenny — saw ragged red edges,
like the bleeding lips of a great wound,
appear, and the machine sank through the
consumed boards into the roaring gulf of
fire beneath. It crashed down, tearing away
posts, ripping beams out of their sockets,
snapping polished rods of steel; and from
where it had vanished came up a volume of

black smoke, charged with a dust of kindled ash.

As the stay for his foot gave way, Hugh slipped and fell. The door burst open, and in rushed Earnshaw, knife in hand, and nearly precipitated himself into the yawning chasm, whence rose the smoke mingled with fire. Hugh was on his feet again in a moment. Annis was at his side. The madman stood and glowered at him; a flame was gnawing into the planks between them, and breaking off portions, and throwing them half consumed into the furnace below.

"Young master's up yonder a long time," said Fawcett. "I think, Gearge, I'll happen go up mysen and see if I can do owt. Wilt 'a hawd up t' stee, lad?"

"Ay, I will. Come thee here, Wilfred, and steady t' stee."

So Fawcett ascended.

"I say, lads," quoth he, looking down, "I hope ya feel mighty humbled in having me lifted over your heads."

"Nay," answered the engineer, with Yorkshire promptitude, "not so long as we've gotten the chance o' pitching thee down, i' our own hands."

"But you've hoisted me to a place whence ya' can't throw me," shouted the irrepressible joker, as he gained the sill.

"Mebbe, you'll find it a middling uncomfortably hot place, yond," retorted Wilfred.

"Happen there's a warmer i' store for thee, lad," bawled Fawcett, before he swung himself into the room.

"Hugh Arkwright, where art thou?"

Hugh shouted in reply, and in a moment Fawcett appeared through the smoke.

" Hold that fiend off, will you ?" cried the young man.

" Why, Joe ! it's never thou ! They say bad pennies is sure to turn up. I think thee's gotten into t' mint again, to be melted up and made into a prettier pictur. Eh, lad ?"

Earnshaw looked at him, and stepping backward into the smoke, disappeared.

" What's he after ?" inquired the lively Fawcett.

" He has gone raving mad," replied Hugh.

Crash. The great entrance door had given way.

They felt it at once. A rush of wind poured in, blowing the fire into redoubled fury, and carrying the flame to the further end of the room with a sudden sweep.

Hugh looked at the stair. The whole aspect of the place was changed. Instead of it serving as a chimney towards which the fire converged, and which drew into it currents of flame, its action was reversed. A blast of cold air poured in at the bottom, and gushed through the open doors on the different landings.

" We can descend, if only we can get the ladder to cross the fallen landing," said Hugh.

" All right!" exclaimed Fawcett. " It's yours in a wink."

He rushed away to the window, and after a little trouble, a good deal of shouting to George and Wilfred, and a few playful sallies, he produced it at the door of the room.

" It's too long," said Fawcett. " Here's t' axe ; shorten it."

It was impossible, without cutting, to make the ladder pass the door. Hugh chopped through the sides with the hatchet Fawcett had brought him from where he had left it, and the two men descended the stone steps. The lower landing was not fallen; it was still on fire, and flaming in places; in others, it was glowing red. The planking had gone, but the rafters remained in a state of combustion, half charcoal, half fire.

Hugh knelt down and tried them with his axe. They were too brittle to support any weight, so he hacked them away, and they fell flaming and crackling to the bottom.

It was cool on the stairs, and an intense relief after the oppressive, parching heat they had endured in the long room. But in safety they were not. The roof above them was blazing, and might fall at any moment. Sparks dropped past them momentarily.

" Down with the ladder," shouted Hugh, as the last rafter of the landing gave way. " Here, give it me." He snatched it from Fawcett's hand, and cast it across the gap as a bridge, one end resting on the lowest step of the upper stair, the other on the topmost step of the other.

" Hold this side," said Fawcett. " Let me go over first. I'll keep it fast at the bottom for thee and t' lass." He walked cautiously along, placing his foot on the rungs, and balancing himself with his arms. The ladder was not quite level, the lower end being some seven inches below the other.

" It's not the pleasantest walk i' t' world," said Fawcett, on reaching a secure footing. " It's like t' Brig o' Dread, nae bigger than a thread, my owd mother used to tell me about. Now, sir, ower wi' t' lass and thee. Cheer up, sweet! don't be flayed."

Outside, Mr. Arkwright waited anxiously. He knew nothing of what had happened to his nephew; he had been told that Hugh and Fawcett were in the mill—that they had entered by one of the windows. He hoped, by bursting in the door, to be able to reach the fire at once, but he was mistaken. The base of the stair and the floor of the hoist were so encumbered with fallen timber, still burning, that when the doors fell in, it seemed probable that they would be in a blaze before they could be dragged out.

But now was heard a heavy rumble, like that of a laden waggon with which the horses had run away. Then a distant cheer, running along from knot to knot of people clustered on the road and watching the blaze. Louder grew the rattle, noisier grew the shouts.

"Here's t' engine at last!" cried Rhodes, as the racing lights became visible, when the machine whirled over the railway bridge and came with horses galloping and foam-splashed, and then dashed through the mill-gates, flung open to receive it.

In two minutes, amidst a thundering cheer, a shoot of water rose up the side of the factory and burst over the roof, to the tramp of the firemen working the engine.

"In yonder," shouted Rhodes. "In at t' door."

"Ay, ay !"

"There are folks there," he cried. "Hand the hose here."

In another moment a volume of water was poured into the great door, and extinguished the fire on the basement.

"Where is Hugh ?" asked Mr. Arkwright. "He can't be in the mill now."

"He's not come out, sir," answered Rhodes. "Lend a hand here, lads; we'll clear them doors and rubbish away, and get t' stairs open."

To return once more to those within.

"Now, sir !" called Fawcett, " I've got fast hold ; lead t' poor little lass along."

Annis put one foot forward, shuddered, and recoiled.

"Oh Hugh, I cannot."

It was a pass of no ordinary danger. Between the bars of the ladder, the eye looked down on smouldering logs, and still blazing fragments of plank, and on the shattered door, lying in the fire, with its splinters already kindled.

It required a steady head, and nerves under control, to cross without turning giddy.

"Annis, you must come," said Hugh.

She looked again and became faint.

"I cannot, indeed. I should fall." Then timidly glancing into his eyes, she asked, "Oh Hugh, could you carry me? I dare not cross that, indeed I dare not."

"Fawcett!" called Hugh. "Do you think this ladder would bear if I carried the girl over?"

"Happen it might, but I can't say."

"Do try, Annis, to go alone."

"Oh I would, I would indeed, but I know I should fall. If there were a plank, I might manage, but a ladder——"

He saw her lips whiten, and a film come over her eyes.

"Then we must do our best. Annis, let me take you in my arms. As once I bore you through flood in safety, so now, please God, I shall bear you through flame." He caught her up, and stepped on the ladder.

"Do not stir," he said. "Pray to God, and be motionless."

He put his feet on the long side poles of the ladder, he did not dare to trust the double weight on the rungs. Moreover, holding Annis, he could not look at his foothold. There was a red spot, a splash of paint, on the wall immediately opposite. He fixed his eyes intently on that as he slowly moved his feet along, sliding each forward, not venturing to raise them.

Then he saw a streak of light at his side, and heard a crash below, as an ignited piece of timber fell from the roof. Immediately after flaming laths flipped out of their places above and went spluttering down.

And next, and more horrible still, he heard a fiendlike yell behind him, and heard the leaping of a man down the stairs at his back. He felt the little girl in his arms tremble.

"Gad! keep off there!" shouted Fawcett, as he saw Earnshaw bound to the head of the ladder, and kick at it, endeavouring to thrust it off the ledge.

Hugh dared not turn his head to look. Determinately he kept his eye on the red stain. The ladder bent under the weight; he knew this by seeing the red spot apparently rise. Suddenly he felt a jar through every fibre of his body. Earnshaw had taken up the axe which Hugh had laid down, and had struck the end of the ladder posts with it. The jerk—as that on which he stood was shot forward a couple of inches—staggered him, and he felt uncertain of his balance. His head swam, and his heart contracted. A blue mist formed before his eyes, and the red patch faded from his vision. An impulse to loosen his grasp of Annis, throw out his arms to steady himself, came over him with scarcely resistible force. It was the natural instinct of self-preservation.

Fawcett saw Earnshaw raise the axe again for a second stroke. He set his own foot against the end of the ladder near him, knowing, however, how impossible it would be for him to resist the jerk of a stroke from the hatchet. He saw the ferocious countenance of the madman blazing with rage and triumph. He saw that one other blow must infallibly shoot the ladder off the step, and send Hugh and his burden into the glowing depths.

Hugh, sickening and faint, pressed a kiss to the cheek of the girl he bore, and her arms tightened around him. Fortunately for him he did not see the uplifted axe, but he heard a rush as of a stream bursting from a sluice, and felt a sharp pang in his hand, and his feet slid along the poles with re-doubled speed. The pain had restored him to full consciousness, the red blotch on the wall became distinct once more. A cry of keen anguish, loud and bewildering from its power of tone and intensity of feeling, pierced his ears. A moment more, and two rough hands clasped him, and he stood with Annis in temporary security.

Still he heard that rushing sound, and still the pealing of those awful cries.

"What is it, what is it?" he gasped.

" Look," answered Fawcett.

Then he saw that the lead cistern on the roof had melted, and was pouring in a glittering cataract upon the steps he had so lately deserted. And there was Earnshaw, writhing in the falling torrent, his face glaring in the flames from above, streaked with silver, his dress coated with glistening metal, with the molten streams rushing on him and leaping off him in shining spirts, uttering burst on burst of shrilling screams, then gathering himself up, and leaping forward, and plunging past them into an abyss of silvery metal and fire and smoke.

"Stand back!" shouted Fawcett.

He caught Hugh and Annis and drew them into the doorway of the willying room. He raised the latch and looked in. The fire seemed to have avoided it, and it was cool and dark. Scarce had they reached it before they heard the rush of water through the entrance door, and its explosion into steam.

" We should ha' been scalded yonder," said Fawcett. " Lucky we got in here."

In another moment the steam, laden with particles of charcoal, and pungent with the odour of wood ash, was swept into the little room, and pervaded it.

The splash and fizz of the water continued, and the room became hot, though the door was shut against the vapour.

" Did you ever hear t' tale," began Fawcett, but stopped; his audience was not disposed to listen. Annis had sunk upon a box in the corner, with her face in her hands, and Hugh was gazing out of the window. Then they heard a shout from below.

Fawcett started to the door. The engine had ceased to play through the entrance, and the stairway was clear of steam at the bottom, though it still hung in a cloud above.

"I think we may venture down," said Fawcett.

Hugh raised Annis gently, and they went out of the willying room.

Now they saw anxious faces looking up through the doorway.

"Who are there?" asked Mr. Arkwright, in a loud voice.

"It's me and Mr. Hugh," replied Fawcett. "And I reckon thy nephew's gone and picked a bird out o' t' flames. Happen a phœnix."

"Come down, will you."

"Ay, we're coming," answered Fawcett. "Look out yonder, there's a dead chap somewhere yonder."

Yes, there he lay, encased in a leaden shroud that glittered like silver, with the steam from the engine water rising from off him.

"Put a board across to t' steps," said

Fawcett, " we ain't a going to walk on hot ashes and scalding lead to please nobody."

" Good heavens !" exclaimed Mr. Arkwright, as the three emerged. " Annis Greenwell."

CHAPTER XVIII.

Miss Doldrums kept her promise. On Saturday she took charge of Annis, moving her to the Lodge, and attending to her. Annis slept the greater part of that day, the anxieties, and the mental and nervous tension of Friday night, having completely exhausted her. Towards evening she recovered, and seemed fresh. Laura brought her to her own room for a talk. She had refrained from questioning Annis before, partly because she had been sound asleep, and partly because Laura had felt the necessity of putting a certain amount of restraint on herself; but now she was determined to satisfy her curiosity, and seeing that Annis looked bright, with the colour in her cheeks, and a light in her eyes, she drew her into her own boudoir, shut the door, seated the girl in a comfortable stool by the fireside, and said—

"Now then, tell me all about it."

"About what?" asked Annis, lifting her wistful eyes.

"About the fire, and Hugh, and the man-monkey, and the watchman, and all that. I am dying to know."

But it was quite beyond the power of Annis to relate the circumstances in a compact and concise form, and she looked at Laura with a despairing expression, that made Miss Doldrums laugh.

"Well, well, begin at the fire," she said.

By degrees the whole story leaked out. Annis could not relate the events of the past night without making allusions to other circumstances which needed explanation, and these in turn opened up other matters which had also to be made clear.

Laura was thus put in possession of the whole story—or very nearly all. Annis had mentioned Hugh as little as possible, and had not referred to their attachment.

"Now then," said Laura, "there is something more I want to know. Yesterday evening Mr. Hugh Arkwright told me that all did not go smoothly between you. You saw him for a moment, I think, and he thought you cold and distant."

Annis hung her head, and did not speak. Laura saw her bosom heave, and her fingers nervously twitch. "Well, dear," said she, "tell me what was the cause of this, I am so eager to know. I take the profoundest interest in all that concerns you and Hugh."

The little girl shrank from disclosing this secret, and still refrained from speaking.

Miss Doldrums went to her side, took her

hands between her own, chafing them
gently, and said again—

"Please to tell me the cause of this.
There is something, is there not?"

"Yes," in a low, tremulous whisper.

"Now tell me what that thing is. You
have not fallen in love with any one else,
have you?"

"Oh, no, no!" looking up suddenly.

"Then what can it be?"

Annis made no answer.

"Has Hugh vexed you in any way?"

"I do not think he cares for me any
more," she said, in a low tone, with her
head bowed down.

"Then I am sure you are out!" exclaimed
Laura. "Why, he is always talking to me
about you. Yesterday evening he asked
me to look after you when you came to
Sowden, and be kind to you. Now I am
doing what I promised him to do."

"Were you at Mr. Arkwright's house last night?" asked Annis, timidly, without raising her head.

"Yes, dear, I was."

"Oh, Miss Doldrums!" began Annis.

"Call me Laura," interrupted the other.

"Joe told me that he had seen Hugh—" She hesitated.

"Doing what?" to help her.

"With another lady." She stopped again.

"Of course, dear, he has to be with heaps of ladies. There is nothing in that."

"But he was kissing her hand, and——"

"Why the fellow, Hugh, did that to me last night. There is nothing in that."

But Annis seemed to think otherwise.

"No," said Laura, sharply, feeling the hands struggling to escape from hers. "No, you misunderstand."

"Joe told me that he had seen Hugh speaking to a lady, looking into her face, full of affection, and she with her eyes raised to his, and her hand clasped in his hands ; and then he bent his head—" There her voice failed her.

"That was me !" exclaimed Laura, with too great precipitation to be careful about her grammar. "Do you know what it was all about ? Look up, Puss."

Annis was unable to do this without revealing the fact that her eyes were full of tears. But one of the glittering drops fell on her knee, and Laura saw it.

"You must dry those silly eyes," said Miss Doldrums. "There is an old saying, Don't cry before you're hurt. That applies to you. You are not hurt in the least, so no crying, please."

"I cannot help it," pleaded Annis.

"Yes, you can. Now listen to me.

Hugh was asking me to befriend you when that awful man saw him.

"I had just promised him that I would take you to stay with me, and he was so grateful, stupid fellow, that he behaved in a foolish way.

"I heard Hugh utter an exclamation, and I saw him start. No doubt he caught a glimpse of the man looking in at him through the front of the conservatory. There!—are you satisfied?"

Annis lifted her face, bright and smiling, in reply. Every cloud was gone.

"You little know how Hugh has talked to me about you. I believe he has no one else in Sowden to whom he can speak about you, so I humour him, and he has told me so much about you that I seem to know you very well."

Annis pressed her hand.

"The great boy has been here to-day, to

inquire after you. I have thought it best that you should not meet to-day, but he is coming here to tea on Sunday, and you can have a nice talk with him then. And your Cousin Martha has been here; you were asleep at the time, so she is going to return somewhat later."

"I should so like to see Martha—dear Martha," said Annis.

"So you shall," answered Laura. "As soon as she comes, she shall be shown up here. I have given orders."

The young women did not continue their conversation for some while. Annis was thinking. When she looked up, she saw that Laura's eyes were fixed on her intently.

"You are so different from me," said Laura.

Annis coloured.

"I suppose I am," she said, with a sigh.

"I feel it myself; and I doubt whether I shall ever be fit for Hugh."

"Fit!" echoed Laura. "Bless the girl! What does she mean?"

"I shall never be like you," said Annis, despondently. "I mean, I shall not be a lady."

"Psh! you are twice as much a lady as I am," exclaimed Laura. "I see my faults clearly, now that I am set alongside of you. You are not harum-scarum, you know."

"Harum-scarum!"

"No, you are not. And it is the great blot in my character that I am so. I am frightfully so. The smoke-jack has got into my constitution, and I twist and twirl all day long. I wish I was not so harum-scarum. If it had not been for the smoke-jack, I should have had to work for my living, and I know I should have been a noisy, pert, giddy girl, who would probably

have come to no good. But money and
education have been my saving. You—you
are quite different. I see it, and I feel it.
You would never be vulgar, rich or poor,
with or without education. I wish I were
like you! Hark. There comes Martha."

CHAPTER XIX.

" Hugh," said Mr. Arkwright, on Monday morning, " where were you yesterday evening ?"

" At church."

" Yes, but before church? We did not see you here at tea."

" I went to Doldrums Lodge. Laura was kind enough to invite me to meet Annis."

" Hold your tongue, sir !" burst forth the manufacturer. " I will not have you mention that girl."

" Then you are still as determined as ever to refuse me your permission to choose a wife for myself."

"No, I do not refuse, so long as that wife is chosen within certain limits."

" Pray mention them."

" An old woman on one side, and a poor one on the other. I do not think, however, that there is much risk of your throwing yourself away on one advanced in years; but young men are reckless about money. They think it will fall upon them out of the clouds, as it did upon—what's her name? Pasiphaë, was it? No—it doesn't matter."

" Danaë, sir."

" Yes, to be sure. Now that shower of gold, in the story of Danaë, was, if I remember aright, a case of matrimony. And I wish young men would just take example from that lady, and look out for an opportunity to form lucrative marriages."

" We had enough of that subject the other evening, I think, uncle. Suppose we give it up as hopeless. Young men are blind, we will suppose, to their monied interest, and are infatuated on the subject of domestic felicity."

" Be hanged to your domestic felicity !" exclaimed Mr. Arkwright. " What does domestic felicity matter to a business man ? He is in his office all day, and he will do well if he attends to his accounts out of business hours. Changing the topic— How the deuce came that girl into the mill ?"

" That is a long story. I have not got to the end of it yet."

" I believe you carried her in there, for the sake of taking her out. I was never more provoked in my life than when I saw her ugly face——"

" It is not ugly."

" I am speaking of the Turk's head. I wish she had been roasted there. That would have been the easiest way of getting out of the difficulty. I suppose, now, you are more obstinate than ever."

" When a man has been through fire and water with a girl, he can hardly do otherwise than I have resolved on doing."

" Well ?"

" I shall certainly make Annis my wife."

" You are a confounded fool. I address my Turk's head."

" It is not in the room."

" It is in my pocket."

" I don't believe it."

" Look, then."

Hugh snatched the pipe from his uncle, and broke the head on the bar of the grate.

" We have had enough of this Turk's head. Please to drop all references to it for the future.'

" Damn !" said Mr. Arkwright. " Hugh, the guilt of my swearing is on your shoulders. You con——"

" The head is off. De mortuis nil nisi bonum."

" Change the topic," grunted the manufacturer.

" To what, sir?"

"Hugh, I am not sorry about the fire. It has done me a world of good. The mill was heavily insured, and now I shall be able to get new machinery. The place, moreover, will be rebuilt, or repaired, and the work is brought to a standstill at a time when trade is at its worst, and when the running of the mill would have entailed loss. I did not like to dismiss my hands—now the fire has relieved me of my difficulty. That maniac could not have done me a better turn, and I am obliged to him. The books are safe. He had not the key of the office, and, as that was detached from the factory, it was unhurt. I'll do the best I can for the man, and bury him decently.

He was not in a club, and has no relations, so that the parish would have to do the job."

"The fellow had money," said Hugh. "It turns out that he had a trifle in a Manchester bank, which brought him in a few pounds interest. His will has been found in his box at the cottage in the Sand Pit. You know he lodged there, and, when he disappeared, his traps remained. Rhodes did not like to disturb them; the cottage belongs to Annis Greenwell, and he did not think he had any right to interfere. But now that the man is undoubtedly dead, his things have been overhauled, and a will, dated a twelvemonth back, has been discovered, leaving all he has to Annis. This is not much—some five-and-twenty pounds a year perhaps—still, it is something."

"And you are going to marry on the strength of this—she being an heiress?" laughed Mr. Arkwright.

Hugh took no notice of his uncle's rudeness. He continued—

"The rest of his things are not worth much. They consist chiefly of books, for the unfortunate fellow was apparently a reading man."

"I could see, from his manner of speaking, that he had some education," said Mr. Arkwright.

"Lately, he has been studying books on insanity and diseases of the brain; at least, so we conclude, for he has quite a library of late works on mental disorders. The poor fellow probably fretted over his disfigurement, and from allowing his mind to prey upon it, he became subject to morbid fancies, and then read himself into a conviction that he was insane. Certainly his acts have not been those of a man with a mind properly balanced; but whether he were actually mad, or only believed himself

to be so, and behaved agreeably to this conviction, is more than I can say."

" Psh!   Mad—of course he was mad."

" I remember once I told you that I
thought he was not right in his mind, and
you disputed my opinion."

" Because it was not grounded on facts.
Here we have a fellow throwing himself
with you into a canal, out of a railway
carriage at full speed."

" The speed was being slackened."

" He thought it was at full speed.   Here,
again, we have a man setting fire to a mill,
with no earthly object except of making a bonfire ; and, like a fool, hampering
the locks beforehand, so that when he tried
to escape from the fire he had raised, he
was unable to do so.   These are facts, and
from them I draw the conclusion that the
man was raving mad."

" I think your facts are not correctly

stated," said Hugh. "My impression is that the poor creature had determined on self-destruction, and, more than that, on making Annis Greenwell perish with him."

"Can you have a clearer evidence of insanity?" asked Mr. Arkwright.

At this moment the door opened, and Sarah Anne looking in, said—

"Please, master, there's a lady wants to see you."

"Show her in," said Mr. Arkwright.

Miss Furness was ushered into the room.

Mr. Arkwright had often met her at the vicarage, but Hugh had not seen her before. He was struck at once with her look and appearance. She was dressed in a silvery grey silk gown, which matched her whitening hair, and contrasted with the pure colour of her transparent complexion. There was something cool and dovelike about her, which charmed him the moment he saw her. He observed the same features as those of the old vicar, but refined and more delicate. Both had the same sweetened expression, caused by much sorrow, and the same serenity of spirit beaming out of every lineament; but in the vicar there was the superadded force of the man, and the consequent deficiency of the tenderness of the woman.

Miss Furness had a pleasant word for Hugh.

"I have often heard of you," she said, "though we have never met."

Then she expressed her sympathy with Mr. Arkwright on account of his terrible loss by the fire, womanlike, supposing that the disaster was very great, and utterly ignorant of the matters beneath the surface, which make an apparent misfortune very often a great advantage. Mr. Arkwright did not un-

deceive het, but hushed her regrets away
with the remark,—

"In trade, you know, there are ups and
downs, and we make our calculations accordingly." Then, suddenly remembering that
he had not inquired after Mrs. Furness, he
repaired the breach of courtesy with charac-
teristic promptitude.

"No news is good news, so I suppose
Mrs. Furness is pretty well?"

"Thank you, yes. She is much the
same, day after day. She has her ups
and downs, too, but not such startling rises
nor such sudden depressions as in your
case. I have got a kind friend to sit with her
to-day during my absence, who will do her
best to amuse her till my return this evening."

"Are you going back so soon?"

"Yes, I must. I have no one who under-
stands my mother to be with her at night.

If little Miss Greenwell had been there, it would have been different."

"Has that girl been with you?" asked Mr. Arkwright, with surprise. "I always supposed she had gone to an orphanage, or a school, or something of that sort."

Hugh smiled. Miss Doldrums had told him the day before to whose care his little girl had been confided by the vicar.

"Yes," answered Miss Furness, "she has been with me, and my mother is so fond of her, that I could safely have trusted the old lady to her; but of course Annis cannot return to York just yet. She is such a sweet child, Mr. Arkwright—don't you think so?"

"Hugh," said the manufacturer, "will you be so good as to see John Rhodes, and tell him to tell me as soon as the insurance fellow comes."

"Yes, sir." Hugh knew that this was a mere excuse to get him out of the room; he, however, took the hint, and left. When he was gone, Mr. Arkwright said—

" My nephew is crazy over that milksop of a girl ; so, when you began praising her, I sent him off."

" She is a very charming little thing," said Miss Furness. " I have seldom met with a better behaved, more simple-minded girl ; she has all the delicacy of feeling that one is glad to find in a well-educated lady, but which is too often wanting."

" I don't care whether she is good or bad," said Mr. Arkwright ; " she is not the sort of person Hugh shall marry."

" I believe the poor child is very fond of him. I have carefully refrained from speaking to her on the subject, but I have seen her colour rise whenever a letter came from Sowden, and then fade, when she found in it no allusion to Hugh. I have observed her very attentively, and I am sure that her whole heart is wrapped up in him, and that her love is not a mere evanescent fancy, but a deep, strong passion."

"You forget, Miss Furness, that her origin is very humble."

"Yes, perhaps I do. But one has only to be with her to forget it at once. Whether it be a crime to be born in a low rank of life, I leave to you to decide. I myself am exceedingly particular about all the proprieties of social life, and I strongly object, on principle, to a marriage out of the sphere in which one is placed by Providence. At the same time I do feel, perhaps I may have had cause to feel, that the mutual devotion of two hearts is too solemn and earnest a feeling to be rudely broken through. Is the humble origin of Annis the sole objection you raise against her?"

"For the matter of that," said Mr. Arkwright, "I do not care so much about her origin as her means. In this manufacturing country, those who are at the bottom of the ladder one day are at the top on the morrow. If you went through Sowden, and picked out only those who could claim a position in the upper ranks of, say two generations, I question whether you would find more than the vicar. Either the father or the grandfather of every one of our aristocracy here have risen from the ranks. No. I am not so particular on that point. But in this money-loving age, and country, and county, one must look for money, and I require Hugh to marry some one with a decent dower, or I shall not take him into partnership. I have already explained my views to him. He knows that he only retains a clerkship if he marries to please himself, but that if he can find a sufficient sum to sink in the business, I make him a partner."

" What do you call a sufficient sum ?"

"Oh, I am not particular; a few thousands."

"If Annis Greenwell had, say eight thousand, would you reject her?"

"Certainly not."

"Then she shall have them."

"Miss Furness!"

"She shall have them," repeated Bessie, with composure. "I do not give them to her, for they do not properly belong to me. But I have money in trust, and I shall be fulfilling that trust if I give them to her."

Mr. Arkwright stared at her with a puzzled air.

Miss Furness continued, quietly — "A gentleman with whom I was intimately acquainted — he was an admiral in the navy——"

"The Silver Poplar!" rudely interrupted Mr. Arkwright, and then at once felt how ill-mannered he had been, and reddened with annoyance.

"The Silver Poplar," repeated Miss Furness, looking him straight in the face, with the softest possible heightening of tinge in her cheek. "Yes, the Silver Poplar left his money to me. He had been saving for many years, and the sum had mounted up. He died, and left all the savings to me—in trust. According to his will, I was his sole legatee; but there were private instructions as to what was to be done with the money, which I have not been able hitherto to carry out. You seem to know something of the history, so I may show you the paper; otherwise, I should only have told you its contents."

"I beg your pardon, Miss Furness," stammered the bewildered man. "I meant no offence."

"I am satisfied of that."

"I had heard something, I own, of your engagement to Admiral Dalmaigne, and I knew, too, the nickname by which he was generally called; and when you mentioned——"

"Make no apology," said Miss Furness, "none is needed. To show you that, so far from being annoyed, I am relieved of an awkwardness by finding you acquainted with the circumstances, I show you, as a friend, this paper." She extended to him a small note. He took it with hesitation, and opened it, and read—

"DEAR BESSIE,

"I leave all my money to you; make use of it as long as you like; but when you want it no more, then employ it to make two young and deserving people happy, whose union is impeded by a barrier such as can be removed by money. It will console me to think that my poor savings, which did not avail us, have comforted others.

"Yours ever,

"WILLIAM DALMAIGNE."

Mr. Arkwright folded up the letter again, and handed it back to Miss Furness, without saying a word.

"I think," continued she, "that you had better say nothing of this to Hugh, nor will I mention it to Annis. I will take the girl back with me to York, where she will be happy, and will be acquiring much that she would not learn among her relatives here. We must let the two write to one another, and we shall see what a year or two will bring forth. If they continue to be attached to one another, then, when suitable, they can marry, but for at least a twelvemonth Annis must remain with me; and I think I can promise you that she will do you no discredit, and that she will make your nephew a faithful and good wife. The money shall be hers as soon as she is married; till then she shall know nothing about it."

Mr. Arkwright did not speak immediately; he was thinking. When he opened his mouth, he had determined to renounce the prospect of having Laura for his niece. " You see, Miss Furness, I had made up my mind that my nephew should marry a certain young lady who has got plenty of money, and I have been trying to force her upon him, with no success. One man may lead a horse to water, but twenty can't make him drink, and though I've brought my Hugh into that same party's society times out of mind, I doubt if all Sowden could make him propose. So I give it up, and I accept your terms. Done."
He held out his hand.

Miss Furness smiled, and extended her fingers.

The manufacturer grasped them, and shook them heartily. "Now," said he, "we are more comfortable. The bargain is struck."

CHAPTER XX.

MORE than two years have slipped by.

It is June. In May, Hugh and Annis were married. And now they come to Sowden, after a month among the lakes.

Hugh introduces his little bride to a sweet cottage, built in the sand pit. The old home of Annis is enlarged and ornamented, and the garden in front stocked with roses in full bloom. The old house and garden have been so transformed, that it is difficult to recognize them again. The cabbage-beds in front have made way for parterres, the "house" window is now that of a little hall. At the side towards the river is a sitting-room with a bow window, and there is a cheerful bedroom over it. Joe's room has been altered into a passage. The cottage is small, but neat and comfortable. In the hall are the stuffed birds, and the white kittens gambol over the kitchen door, but General Garibaldi has disappeared.

The little wife looks round, with a flutter of delight.

"Oh, Hugh!" she says, putting her hands on his shoulders, and looking up into his face. "I want to ask one favour."

"Wait," he says. Then he draws forth a crimson kerchief, and puts it over her head, makes her pin it under her chin, and look up blushing at Ifim.

"Now, Annis, what do you want?"

"Oh, Hugh! I wish you would let Martha come and live with us?"

"Martha!" shouted Hugh.

The kitchen door opened, and Martha came in. With a cry of delight, the bride flew from her husband, to the arms of her cousin.

"There, that is sufficient," said Hugh. "I alone have been through Flood and Flame with you, so come back to me."

THE END.

LONDON : PRINTED BY WILLIAM CLOWES AND SONS, STAMFORD STREET
AND CHARING CROSS.

www.ingramcontent.com/pod-product-compliance
Lightning Source LLC
Chambersburg PA
CBHW060555030726
47498CB00005B/1406